Collector's Library

THE TURN OF THE SCREW
and
OWEN WINGRAVE

THE TURN OF
THE SCREW
&
OWEN WINGRAVE

Afterword by
DAVID STUART DAVIES

Collector's Library

The Turn of the Screw was first published in 1898.
Owen Wingrave was first published in 1893.
This edition published in 2011 by
Collector's Library
an imprint of CRW Publishing Limited
69 Gloucester Crescent, London NW1 7EG

ISBN   978 1 907360 32 9

Text and Introduction copyright ©
CRW Publishing Limited 2011

Typeset in Great Britain by Antony Gray
Printed and bound in China by Imago

1

CONTENTS

CONTENTS

THE TURN
OF THE SCREW

PROLOGUE

The story had held us, round the fire, sufficiently breathless, but except the obvious remark that it was gruesome, as on Christmas Eve in an old house a strange tale should essentially be, I remember no comment uttered till somebody happened to note it as the only case he had met in which such a visitation had fallen on a child. The case, I may mention, was that of an apparition in just such an old house as had gathered us for the occasion – an appearance, of a dreadful kind, to a little boy sleeping in the room with his mother and waking her up in the terror of it; waking her not to dissipate his dread and soothe him to sleep again, but to encounter also herself, before she had succeeded in doing so, the same sight that had shocked him. It was this observation that drew from Douglas – not immediately, but later in the evening – a reply that had the interesting consequence to which I call attention. Someone else told a story not particularly effective, which I saw he was not following. This I took for a sign that he had himself something to produce and that we should only have to wait. We waited in fact till two nights later; but that same evening, before we scattered, he brought out what was in his mind.

'I quite agree – in regard to Griffin's ghost, or whatever it was – that its appearing first to the little boy, at so tender an age, adds a particular touch. But it's not the first occurrence of its charming kind that I know to have been concerned with a child. If the child gives the effect another turn of the screw, what do you say to *two* children – ?'

'We say, of course,' somebody exclaimed, 'that two children give two turns! Also that we want to hear about them.'

I can see Douglas there before the fire, to which he had got up to present his back, looking down at this converser with his hands in his pockets. 'Nobody but me, till now, has ever heard. It's quite too horrible.' This was naturally declared by several voices to give the thing the utmost price, and our friend, with quiet art, prepared his triumph by turning his eyes over the rest of us and going on: 'It's beyond everything. Nothing at all that I know touches it.'

'For sheer terror?' I remember asking.

He seemed to say it wasn't so simple as that; to be really at a loss how to qualify it. He passed his hand over his eyes, made a little wincing grimace. 'For dreadful – dreadfulness!'

'Oh, how delicious!' cried one of the women.

He took no notice of her; he looked at me, but as if, instead of me, he saw what he spoke of. 'For general uncanny ugliness and horror and pain.'

'Well, then,' I said, 'just sit right down and begin.'

He turned round to the fire, gave a kick to a log, watched it an instant. Then as he faced us again: 'I can't begin. I shall have to send to town.' There was a unanimous groan at this, and much reproach; after which, in his preoccupied way, he explained. 'The story's written. It's in a locked drawer – it has not been out for years. I could write to my man and enclose the key; he could send down the packet as he finds it.' It was to me in particular that he appeared to propound this – appeared almost to appeal for aid not to hesitate. He had broken a thickness of ice, the formation of many a winter; had had his reasons for a long silence. The others resented postponement, but it was just his scruples that charmed me. I adjured him to write by the first post and to agree with us for an early hearing; then I asked him if the experience in question had been his own. To this his answer was prompt. 'Oh, thank God, no!'

'And is the record yours? You took the thing down?'

'Nothing but the impression. I took that *here*' – he tapped his heart. 'I've never lost it.'

'Then your manuscript – ?'

'Is in old faded ink and in the most beautiful hand.' He hung fire again. 'A woman's. She has been dead these twenty years. She sent me the pages in question before she died.' They were all listening now, and of course there was somebody to be arch, or at any rate to draw the inference. But if he put the inference by without a smile it was also without irritation. 'She was a most charming person, but she was ten years older than I. She was my sister's governess,' he quietly said. 'She was the most agreeable woman I've ever known in her position; she would have been worthy of any whatever. It was long ago, and this episode was long before. I was at Trinity, and I found her at home on my coming down the second summer. I was much there that year – it was a beautiful one; and we had, in her off-hours, some strolls and talks in the garden – talks in which she struck me as awfully clever and nice. Oh, yes; don't grin: I liked her extremely and am glad to this day to think she liked me too. If she hadn't she wouldn't have told me. She had never told anyone. It wasn't simply that she said so, but that I knew she hadn't. I was sure; I could see. You'll easily judge why when you hear.'

'Because the thing had been such a scare?'

He continued to fix me. 'You'll easily judge,' he repeated; '*you* will.'

I fixed him too. 'I see. She was in love.'

He laughed for the first time. 'You *are* acute. Yes, she was in love. That is, she *had* been. That came out – she couldn't tell her story without its coming out. I saw it, and she saw I saw it; but neither of us spoke of it. I remember the time and the place – the corner of the lawn, the shade of the great beeches and the long hot summer afternoon. It wasn't a scene for a shudder; but oh – !' He quitted the fire and dropped back into his chair.

'You'll receive the packet Thursday morning?' I said.

'Probably not till the second post.'

'Well then; after dinner – '

'You'll all meet me here?' He looked us round again. 'Isn't anybody going?' It was almost the tone of hope.

'Everybody will stay!'

'*I* will – and *I* will!' cried the ladies whose departure had been fixed. Mrs Griffin, however, expressed the need for a little more light. 'Who was it she was in love with?'

'The story will tell,' I took upon myself to reply.

'Oh, I can't wait for the story!'

'The story *won't* tell,' said Douglas; 'not in any literal, vulgar way.'

'More's the pity then. That's the only way I ever understand.'

'Won't *you* tell, Douglas?' somebody else inquired.

He sprang to his feet again. 'Yes – tomorrow. Now I must go to bed. Good-night.' And, quickly catching up a candlestick, he left us slightly bewildered. From our end of the great brown hall we heard his step on the stair; whereupon Mrs Griffin spoke. 'Well, if I don't know who she was in love with I know who *he* was.'

'She was ten years older,' said her husband.

'*Raison de plus* – at that age! But it's rather nice, his long reticence.'

'Forty years!' Griffin put in.

'With this outbreak at last.'

'The outbreak,' I returned, 'will make a tremendous occasion of Thursday night'; and everyone so agreed with me that in the light of it we lost all attention for everything else. The last story, however incomplete and like the mere opening of a serial, had been told; we handshook and 'candlestuck', as somebody said, and went to bed.

I knew the next day that a letter containing the key had, by the first post, gone off to his London apartments; but in spite of – or perhaps just on account of – the eventual diffusion of this knowledge we quite let him alone till after dinner, till such an hour of the evening in fact as might best accord with the kind of emotion on which our hopes were fixed. Then he became as communicative as we could desire, and indeed gave us his best reason for being so. We had it from him again before the fire in the hall, as we had had our mild wonders of the previous night. It appeared that the narrative he had promised to read us really required for a proper intelligence a few words of prologue. Let me say here distinctly, to have done with it, that this narrative, from an exact transcript of my own made much later, is what I shall presently give. Poor Douglas, before his death – when it was in sight – committed to me the manuscript that reached him on the third of these days and that, on the same spot, with immense effect, he began to read to our hushed little circle on the night of the fourth. The departing ladies who had said they would stay didn't, of course, thank heaven, stay: they departed, in consequence of arrangements made, in a rage of curiosity, as they professed, produced by the touches with which he had already worked us up. But that only made his little final auditory more compact and select, kept it round the hearth subject to a common thrill.

The first of these touches conveyed that the written statement took up the date at a point after it had, in a manner, begun. The fact to be in possession of was therefore that his old friend, the youngest of several daughters of a poor country parson, had at the age of twenty, on taking service for the first time in the schoolroom, come up to London, in trepidation, to answer in person an advertisement that had already placed her in brief correspondence with the advertiser. This person proved, on her presenting herself for judgement at a house in Harley Street that impressed her as vast and imposing – this prospective patron proved a gentleman, a bachelor in the prime of life, such a figure as had never risen, save in a dream or an old novel, before a fluttered, anxious girl out of a Hampshire vicarage. One could easily fix his type; it never, happily, dies out. He was handsome and bold and pleasant, offhand and gay and kind. He struck her, inevitably, as gallant and splendid, but what took her most of all and gave her the courage she after-wards showed was that he put the whole thing to her as a favour, an obligation he should gratefully incur. She figured him as rich, but as fearfully extravagant – saw him all in a glow of high fashion, of good looks, of expensive habits, of charming ways with women. He had for his town residence a big house filled with the spoils of travel and the trophies of the chase; but it was to his country home, an old family place in Essex, that he wished her immediately to proceed.

He had been left, by the death of their parents in India, guardian to a small nephew and a small niece, children of a younger, a military brother whom he had lost two years before. These children were, by the strangest of chances for a man in his position – a lone man without the right sort of experience or a grain of patience – very heavy on his hands. It had all been a great worry and, on his own part doubtless, a series of blunders, but he immensely pitied the poor chicks and had done all he could; had in particular sent them down to his other house, the proper place for them being of course the country, and kept them there from the first with the best people he could find to look after them, parting even with his own servants to wait on them and going down himself, whenever he might, to see how they were doing. The awkward thing was that they had practically no other relations and that his own affairs took up all his time. He had put them in possession of Bly, which was healthy and secure, and had placed at the head of their little establishment – but below stairs only – an excellent woman, Mrs Grose, whom he was sure his visitor would like and who had formerly been maid to his mother. She was now housekeeper and was also acting for the time as superintendent to the little girl, of whom, without children of her own, she was by good luck extremely fond. There were plenty of people to help, but of course the young lady who should go down as governess would be in supreme authority. She would also have, in holidays, to look after the small boy, who had been for a term at school – young as he was to be sent, but what else could be done? – and who, as the holidays were about to begin, would be back from one day to the other. There had been for the two children at first a young lady, whom they had had the misfortune to lose. She had done for them quite beautifully – she was a most respectable person – till her death, the great awkwardness of which had, precisely, left no alternative but the school for little Miles. Mrs Grose, since then, in the way of manners and things, had done as she could for Flora; and there were further, a cook, a housemaid, a dairywoman, an old pony, an old groom and an old gardener, all likewise thoroughly respectable.

So far had Douglas presented his picture when someone put a question. 'And what did the former governess die of? Of so much respectability?'

Our friend's answer was prompt. 'That will come out. I don't anticipate.'

'Pardon me – I thought that was just what you *are* doing.'

'In her successor's place,' I suggested, 'I should have wished to learn if the office brought with it – '

'Necessary danger to life?' Douglas completed my thought. 'She did wish to learn, and she did learn. You shall hear tomorrow what she learnt. Meanwhile of course the prospect struck her as slightly grim. She was young, untried, nervous: it was a vision of serious duties and little company, of really great loneliness.

She hesitated – took a couple of days to consult and consider. But the salary offered much exceeded her modest measure, and on a second interview she faced the music, she engaged.' And Douglas, with this, made a pause that, for the benefit of the company, moved me to throw in: 'The moral of which was of course the seduction exercised by the splendid young man. She succumbed to it.'

He got up and, as he had done the night before, went to the fire, gave a stir to a log with his foot, then stood a moment with his back to us. 'She saw him only twice.'

'Yes, but that's just the beauty of her passion.'

A little to my surprise, on this, Douglas turned round to me. 'It *was* the beauty of it. There were others,' he went on, 'who hadn't succumbed. He told her frankly all his difficulty – that for several applicants the conditions had been prohibitive. They were somehow simply afraid. It sounded dull – it sounded strange; and all the more so because of his main condition.'

'Which was – ?'

'That she should never trouble him – but never, never: neither appeal nor complain nor write about anything; only meet all questions herself, receive all moneys from his solicitor, take the whole thing over and let him alone. She promised to do this, and she mentioned to me that when, for a moment, disburdened, delighted, he held her hand, thanking her for the sacrifice, she already felt rewarded.'

'But was that all her reward?' one of the ladies asked.

'She never saw him again.'

'Oh!' said the lady; which, as our friend immediately

again left us, was the only other word of importance contributed to the subject till, the next night, by the corner of the hearth, in the best chair, he opened the faded red cover of a thin, old-fashioned, gilt-edged album. The whole thing took indeed more nights than one, but on the first occasion the same lady put another question. 'What's your title?'

'I haven't one.'

'Oh, *I* have!' I said. But Douglas, without heeding me, had begun to read with a fine clearness that was like a rendering to the ear of the beauty of his author's hand.

I remember the whole beginning as a succession of flights and drops, a little seesaw of the right throbs and the wrong. After rising, in town, to meet his appeal I had at all events a couple of very bad days – found all my doubts bristle again, felt indeed sure I had made a mistake. In this state of mind I spent the long hours of bumping swinging coach that carried me to the stopping-place at which I was to be met by a vehicle from the house. This convenience, I was told, had been ordered, and I found, towards the close of the June afternoon, a commodious fly in waiting for me. Driving at that hour, on a lovely day, through a country the summer sweetness of which served as a friendly welcome, my fortitude revived and, as we turned into the avenue, took a flight that was probably but a proof of the point to which it had sunk. I suppose I had expected, or had dreaded, something so dreary that what greeted me was a good surprise. I remember as a thoroughly pleasant impression the broad, clear front, its open windows and fresh curtains and the pair of maids looking out; I remember the lawn and the bright flowers and the crunch of my wheels on the gravel and the clustered treetops over which the rooks circled and cawed in the golden sky. The scene had a greatness that made it a different affair from my own scant home, and there immediately appeared at the door, with a little girl in her hand, a civil person who dropped me as decent a curtsy as if I had been the mistress or a distinguished visitor. I had received in Harley Street a narrower notion of the place, and that, as I recalled it, made me think the proprietor still more of a gentleman, suggested that what I was to enjoy might be a matter beyond his promise.

I had no drop again till the next day, for I was carried triumphantly through the following hours by my introduction to the younger of my pupils. The little girl who accompanied Mrs Grose affected me on the spot as a creature too charming not to make it a great fortune to have to do with her. She was the most beautiful child I had ever seen, and I afterwards wondered why my employer hadn't made more of a point to me of this. I slept little that night – I was too much excited; and this astonished me too, I recollect, remained with me, adding to my sense of the liberality with which I was treated. The large, impressive room, one of the best in the house, the great state bed as I almost felt it, the figured full curtains, the long glasses in which, for the first time, I could see myself from head to foot, all struck me – like the wonderful appeal of my small charge – as so many things thrown in. It was thrown in as well, from the first moment, that I should get on with Mrs Grose in a relation over which, on my way, in the coach, I fear I had rather brooded. The one appearance indeed that in this early outlook might have made me shrink again was that of her being so inordinately glad to see me. I felt within half an hour that she was so glad – stout, simple, plain, clean, wholesome woman – as to be positively on her guard against showing it too much. I wondered even then a little why she should wish *not* to show it, and that, with reflection, with suspicion, might of course have made me uneasy.

But it was a comfort that there could be no un-easiness in a connection with anything so beatific as the radiant image of my little girl, the vision of whose angelic beauty had probably more than anything else to do with the restlessness that, before morning, made me several times rise and wander about my room to take in the whole picture and prospect; to watch from my open window the faint summer dawn, to look at such stretches of the rest of the house as I could catch, and to listen, while in the fading dusk the first birds began to twitter, for the possible recurrence of a sound or two, less natural and not without but within, that I had fancied I heard. There had been a moment when I believed I recognised, faint and far, the cry of a child; there had been another when I found myself just consciously starting as at the passage, before my door, of a light footstep. But these fancies were not marked enough not to be thrown off, and it is only in the light, or the gloom, I should rather say, of other and subsequent matters that they now come back to me. To watch, teach, 'form' little Flora would too evidently be the making of a happy and useful life. It had been agreed between us downstairs that after this first occasion I should have her as a matter of course at night, her small white bed being already arranged, to that end, in my room. What I had undertaken was the whole care of her, and she had remained just this last time with Mrs Grose only as an effect of our consideration for my inevitable strangeness and her natural timidity. In spite of this timidity – which the child herself, in the oddest way in the world, had been perfectly frank and brave about, allowing it, without a sign of uncomfortable consciousness, with the deep, sweet serenity indeed of one of Raphael's holy infants, to be discussed, to be imputed to her and to determine us – I felt quite sure she would presently like me. It was part of what I already liked Mrs Grose herself for, the pleasure I could see her feel in my admiration and wonder as I sat at supper with four tall candles and with my pupil, in a high chair and a bib, brightly facing me between them over bread and milk. There were naturally things that in Flora's presence could pass between us only as prodigious and gratified looks, obscure and round-about allusions.

'And the little boy – does he look like her? Is he, too, so very remarkable?'

One wouldn't, it was already conveyed between us, too grossly flatter a child. 'Oh, miss, *most* remarkable. If you think well of this one!' – and she stood there with a plate in her hand, beaming at our companion, who looked from one of us to the other with placid, heavenly eyes that contained nothing to check us.

'Yes; if I do – ?'

'You *will* be carried away by the little gentleman!'

'Well, that, I think, is what I came for – to be carried away. I'm afraid, however,' I remember feeling the impulse to add, 'I'm rather easily carried away. I was carried away in London!'

I can still see Mrs Grose's broad face as she took this in.

'In Harley Street?'

'In Harley Street.'

'Well, miss, you're not the first – and you won't be the last.'

'Oh, I've no pretensions,' I could laugh, 'to being the only one. My other pupil, at any rate, as I under-stand, comes back tomorrow?'

'Not tomorrow – Friday, miss. He arrives, as you did, by the coach, under care of the guard, and is to be met by the same carriage.'

I forthwith wanted to know if the proper as well as the pleasant and friendly thing wouldn't therefore be that on the arrival of the public conveyance I should await him with his little sister; a proposition to which Mrs Grose assented so heartily that I somehow took her manner as a kind of comforting pledge – never falsified, thank heaven! – that we should on every question be quite at one. Oh, she was glad I was there!

What I felt the next day was, I suppose, nothing that could be fairly called a reaction from the cheer of my arrival; it was probably at the most only a slight oppression produced by a fuller measure of the scale, as I walked round them, gazed up at them, took them in, of my new circumstances. They had, as it were, an extent and mass for which I had not been prepared and in the presence of which I found myself, freshly, a little scared, not less than a little proud. Regular lessons, in this agitation, certainly suffered some wrong; I reflected that my first duty was, by the gentlest arts I could contrive, to win the child into the sense of knowing me. I spent the day with her out of doors; I arranged with her, to her great satisfaction, that it should be she, she only, who might show me the place. She showed it step by step and room by room and secret by secret, with droll, delightful, childish talk about it, and with the result, in half an hour, of our becoming tremendous friends. Young as she was I was struck, throughout our little tour, with her confidence and courage, with the way, in empty chambers and dull corridors, on crooked staircases that made me pause, and even on the summit of an old machicolated square tower that made me dizzy, her morning music, her disposition to tell me so many more things than she asked, rang out and led me on. I have not seen Bly since the day I left it, and I dare say that to my present older and more informed eyes it would show a very reduced importance. But as my little conductress, with her hair of gold and her frock of blue, danced before me round corners and pattered down passages, I had the view of a castle of romance inhabited by a rosy sprite, such a place as would somehow, for diversion of the young idea, take all colour out of storybooks and fairytales. Wasn't it just a storybook over which I had fallen a-doze and a-dream? No: it was a big, ugly, antique but convenient house, embodying a few features of a building still older, half-displaced and half-utilised, in which I had the fancy of our being almost as lost as a handful of passengers in a great drifting ship. Well, I was strangely at the helm!

CHAPTER 2

This came home to me when, two days later, I drove over with Flora to meet, as Mrs Grose said, the little gentleman; and all the more for an incident that, presenting itself the second evening, had deeply disconcerted me. The first day had been, on the whole, as I have expressed, reassuring; but I was to see it wind up to a change of note. The postbag that evening – it came late – contained a letter for me which, however, in the hand of my employer, I found to be composed but of a few words enclosing another, addressed to himself, with a seal still unbroken. 'This, I recognise, is from the headmaster, and the headmaster's an awful bore. Read him, please; deal with him; but mind you don't report. Not a word. I'm off!' I broke the seal with a great effort – so great a one that I was a long time coming to it; took the unopened missive at last up to my room and only attacked it just before going to bed. I had better have let it wait till morning, for it gave me a second sleepless night. With no counsel to take, the next day, I was full of distress; and it finally got so the better of me that I determined to open myself at least to Mrs Grose.

'What does it mean? The child's dismissed his school.'

She gave me a look that I remarked at the moment; then, visibly, with a quick blankness, seemed to try to take it back. 'But aren't they all – ?'

'Sent home – yes. But only for the holidays. Miles may never go back at all.'

Consciously, under my attention, she reddened. 'They won't take him?'

'They absolutely decline.'

At this she raised her eyes, which she had turned from me; I saw them fill with good tears. 'What has he done?'

I cast about; then I judged best simply to hand her my document – which, however, had the effect of making her, without taking it, simply put her hands behind her. She shook her head sadly. 'Such things are not for me, miss.'

My counsellor couldn't read! I winced at my mistake, which I attenuated as I could, and opened the letter again to repeat it to her; then, faltering in the act and folding it up once more, I put it back in my pocket. 'Is it really *bad*?'

The tears were still in her eyes. 'Do the gentlemen say so?'

'They go into no particulars. They simply express their regret that it should be impossible to keep him. That can have but one meaning.' Mrs Grose listened with dumb emotion; she forbore to ask me what this meaning might be; so that, presently, to put the thing with some coherence and with the mere aid of her presence to my own mind, I went on: 'That he's an injury to the others.'

At this, with one of the quick turns of simple folk, she suddenly flamed up. 'Master Miles! – *him* an injury?'

There was such a flood of good faith in it that, though I had not yet seen the child, my very fears made me jump to the absurdity of the idea. I found myself, to meet my friend the better, offering it, on the spot, sarcastically. 'To his poor little innocent mates!'

'It's too dreadful,' cried Mrs Grose, 'to say such cruel things! Why, he's scarce ten years old.'

'Yes, yes; it would be incredible.'

She was evidently grateful for such a profession. 'See him, miss, first. *Then* believe it!' I felt forthwith a new impatience to see him; it was the beginning of a curiosity that, all the next hours, was to deepen almost to pain. Mrs Grose was aware, I could judge, of what she had produced in me, and she followed it up with assurance. 'You might as well believe it of the little lady. Bless her,' she added the next moment – '*look* at her!'

I turned and saw that Flora, whom, ten minutes

before, I had established in the schoolroom with a sheet of white paper, a pencil and a copy of nice 'round O's', now presented herself to view at the open door. She expressed in her little way an extraordinary detachment from disagreeable duties, looking at me, however, with a great childish light that seemed to offer it as a mere result of the affection she had conceived for my person, which had rendered necessary that she should follow me. I needed nothing more than this to feel the full force of Mrs Grose's comparison, and, catching my pupil in my arms, covered her with kisses in which there was a sob of atonement.

None the less, the rest of the day, I watched for further occasion to approach my colleague, especially as, towards evening, I began to fancy she rather sought to avoid me. I overtook her, I remember, on the staircase; we went down together and at the bottom I detained her, holding her there with a hand on her arm. 'I take what you said to me at noon as a declaration that you've never known him to be bad.'

She threw back her head; she had clearly by this time, and very honestly, adopted an attitude. 'Oh, never known him – I don't pretend *that*!'

I was upset again. 'Then you *have* known him – ?'

'Yes indeed, miss, thank God!'

On reflection I accepted this. 'You mean that a boy who never is – ?'

'Is no boy for *me*!'

I held her tighter. 'You like them with the spirit to be naughty?' Then, keeping pace with her answer, 'So do I!' I eagerly brought out. 'But not to the degree to contaminate – '

'To contaminate?' – my big word left her at a loss.

I explained it. 'To corrupt.'

She stared, taking my meaning in; but it produced in her an odd laugh. 'Are you afraid he'll corrupt *you*?' She put the question with such a fine bold humour that with a laugh, a little silly doubtless, to match her own, I gave way for the time to the apprehension of ridicule.

But the next day, as the hour for my drive approached, I cropped up in another place. 'What was the lady who was here before?'

'The last governess? She was also young and pretty – almost as young and almost as pretty, miss, even as you.'

'Ah, then I hope her youth and her beauty helped her!' I recollect throwing off. 'He seems to like us young and pretty!'

'Oh, he *did*,' Mrs Grose assented; 'It was the way he liked everyone!' She had no sooner spoken, indeed, than she caught herself up. 'I mean that's his way – the master's.'

I was struck. 'But of whom did you speak first?'

She looked blank, but she coloured. 'Why, of *him*.'

'Of the master?'

'Of who else?'

There was so obviously no one else that the next moment I had lost my impression of her having accidentally said more than she meant; and I merely asked what I wanted to know. 'Did *she* see anything in the boy – ?'

'That wasn't right? She never told me.'

I had a scruple, but I overcame it. 'Was she careful – particular?'

Mrs Grose appeared to try to be conscientious. 'About some things – yes.'

'But not about all?'

Again she considered. 'Well, miss – she's gone. I won't tell tales.'

'I quite understand your feeling,' I hastened to reply; but I thought it after an instant not opposed to this concession to pursue: 'Did she die here?'

'No – she went off.'

I don't know what there was in this brevity of Mrs Grose's that struck me as ambiguous. 'Went off to die?' Mrs Grose looked straight out of the window, but I felt that, hypothetically, I had a right to know what young persons engaged for Bly were expected to do. 'She was taken ill, you mean, and went home?'

'She was not taken ill, so far as appeared, in this house. She left it, at the end of the year, to go home, as she said, for a short holiday, to which the time she had put in had certainly given her a right. We had then a young woman – a nursemaid who had stayed on and who was a good girl and clever; and *she* took the children altogether for the interval. But our young lady never came back, and at the very moment I was expecting her I heard from the master that she was dead.'

I turned this over. 'But of what?'

'He never told me! But please, miss,' said Mrs Grose, 'I must get to my work.'

CHAPTER 3

Her thus turning her back on me was fortunately not, for my just preoccupations, a snub that could check the growth of our mutual esteem. We met, after I had brought home little Miles, more intimately than ever on the ground of my stupefaction, my general emotion: so monstrous was I then ready to pronounce it that such a child as had now been revealed to me should be under an interdict. I was a little late on the scene of his arrival, and I felt, as he stood wistfully looking out for me before the door of the inn at which the coach had put him down, that I had seen him on the instant, without and within, in the great glow of freshness, the same positive fragrance of purity, in which I had from the first moment seen his little sister. He was incredibly beautiful, and Mrs Grose had put her finger on it: everything but a sort of passion of tenderness for him was swept away by his presence. What I then and there took him to my heart for was something divine that I have never found to the same degree in any child – his indescribable little air of knowing nothing in the world but love. It would have been impossible to carry a bad name with a greater sweetness of innocence, and by the time I had got back to Bly with him I remained merely bewildered – so far, that is, as I was not outraged – by the sense of the horrible letter locked up in one of the drawers in my room. As soon as I could compass a private word with Mrs Grose, I declared to her that it was grotesque.

She promptly understood me. 'You mean the cruel charge – ?'

'It doesn't live an instant. My dear woman, look at him!'

She smiled at my pretension to have discovered his charm. 'I assure you, miss, I do nothing else! What will you say then?' she immediately added.

'In answer to the letter?' I had made up my mind. 'Nothing at all.'

'And to his uncle?'

I was incisive. 'Nothing at all.'

'And to the boy himself?'

I was wonderful. 'Nothing at all.'

She gave with her apron a great wipe to her mouth. 'Then I'll stand by you. We'll see it out.'

'We'll see it out!' I ardently echoed, giving her my hand to make it a vow.

She held me there a moment, then whisked up her apron again with her detached hand. 'Would you mind, miss, if I used the freedom – '

'To kiss me? No!' I took the good creature in my arms and, after we had embraced like sisters, felt still more fortified and indignant.

This, at all events, was for the time: a time so full that as I recall the way it went it reminds me of all the art I now need to make it a little distinct. What I look back at with amazement is the situation I accepted. I had undertaken, with my companion, to see it out, and I was under a charm apparently that could smooth away the extent and the far and difficult connections of such an effort. I was lifted aloft on a great wave of infatuation and pity. I found it simple, in my ignorance, my confusion and perhaps my conceit, to assume that I could deal with a boy whose education for the world was all on the point of beginning. I am unable even to remember at this day what proposal I framed for the end of his holidays and the resumption of his studies. Lessons with me indeed, that charming summer, we all had a theory that he was to have; but I now feel that for weeks the lessons must have been rather my own. I learnt something – at first certainly – that had not been one of the teachings of my small, smothered life; learnt to be amused, and even amusing, and not to think for the morrow. It was the first time, in a manner, that I had known space and air and freedom, all the music of summer and all the mystery of nature. And then there was consideration – and consideration was sweet. Oh, it was a trap – not designed but deep – to my imagination, to my delicacy, perhaps to my vanity; to whatever in me was most excitable. The best way to picture it all is to say that I was off my guard. They gave me so little trouble – they were of a gentleness so extraordinary. I used to speculate – but even this with a dim disconnectedness – as to how the rough future (for all futures are rough!) would handle them and might bruise them. They had the bloom of health and happiness; and yet, as if I had been in charge of a pair of little grandees, of princes of the blood, for whom everything, to be right, would have to be fenced about and ordered and arranged, the only form that in my fancy the after-years could take for them was that of a romantic, a really royal extension of the garden and the park. It may be of course above all what suddenly broke into this gives the previous time a charm of stillness – that hush in which something gathers or crouches. The change was actually like the spring of a beast.

In the first weeks, the days were long; they often, at their finest, gave me what I used to call my own hour, the hour when, for my pupils, teatime and bedtime having come and gone, I had before my final retirement a small interval alone. Much as I liked my companions, this hour was the thing in the day I liked most; and I liked it best of all when, as the light faded – or rather, I should say, the day lingered and the last calls of the last birds sounded, in a flushed sky, from the old trees – I could take a turn into the grounds and enjoy, almost with a sense of property that amused and flattered me, the beauty and dignity of the place. It was a pleasure at these moments to feel myself tranquil and justified; doubtless perhaps also to reflect that by my discretion, my quiet good sense and general high propriety, I was giving pleasure – if he ever thought of it! – to the person to whose pressure I had yielded. What I was doing was what he had earnestly hoped and directly asked of me, and that I *could*, after all, do it proved even a greater joy than I had expected. I dare say I fancied myself, in short, a remarkable young woman and took comfort in the faith that this would more publicly appear. Well, I needed to be remarkable to offer a front to the remarkable things that presently gave their first sign.

It was plump, one afternoon, in the middle of my very hour: the children were tucked away and I had come out for my stroll. One of the thoughts that, as I don't in the least shrink now from noting, used to be with me in these wanderings was that it would be as charming as a charming story suddenly to meet some-one. Someone would appear there at the turn of a path and would stand before me and smile and approve. I didn't ask more than that – I only asked that he should know; and the only way to be sure he knew would be to see it, and the kind light of it, in his handsome face. That was exactly present to me – by which I mean the face was – when, on the first of these occasions, at the end of a long June day, I stopped short on emerging from one of the plantations and coming into view of the house. What arrested me on the spot – and with a shock much greater than any

33

vision had allowed for – was the sense that my imagination had, in a flash, turned real. He did stand there! – but high up, beyond the lawn and at the very top of the tower to which, on that first morning, little Flora had conducted me. This tower was one of a pair – square, incongruous, crenellated structures – that were distinguished, for some reason, though I could see little difference, as the new and the old. They flanked opposite ends of the house and were probably architectural absurdities, redeemed in a measure, indeed, by not being wholly disengaged nor of a height too pretentious, dating, in their gingerbread antiquity, from a romantic revival that was already a respectable past. I admired them, had fancies about them, for we could all profit in a degree, especially when they loomed through the dusk, by the grandeur of their actual battlements; yet it was not at such an elevation that the figure I had so often invoked seemed most in place.

It produced in me, this figure, in the clear twilight, I remember, two distinct gasps of emotion, which were, sharply, the shock of my first and that of my second surprise. My second was a violent perception of the mistake of my first: the man who met my eyes was not the person I had precipitately supposed. There came to me thus a bewilderment of vision of which, after these years, there is no living view that I can hope to give. An unknown man in a lonely place is a permitted object of fear to a young woman privately bred; and the figure that faced me was – a few more seconds assured me – as little anyone else I knew as it was the image that had been in my mind. I had not seen it in Harley Street – I had not seen it anywhere. The place, moreover, in the strangest way in the world, had on the instant and by the very fact of its appearance become a solitude. To me at least, making my statement here with a deliberation with which I have never made it, the whole feeling of the moment returns. It was as if, while I took in what I did take in, all the rest of the scene had been stricken with death. I can hear again, as I write, the intense hush in which the sounds of evening dropped. The rooks stopped cawing in the golden sky and the friendly hour lost for the unspeakable minute all its voice. But there was no other change in nature, unless indeed it were a change that I saw with a stranger sharpness. The gold was still in the sky, the clearness in the air, and the man who looked at me over the battlements was as definite as a picture in a frame. That's how I thought, with extraordinary quickness, of each person he might have been and that he wasn't. We were confronted across our distance quite long enough for me to ask myself with intensity who then he was and to feel, as an effect of my inability to say, a wonder that in a few seconds more became intense.

The great question, or one of these, is afterwards, I know, with regard to certain matters, the question of how long they have lasted. Well, this matter of mine, think what you will of it, lasted while I caught at a dozen possibilities, none of which made a difference for the better, that I could see, in there having been in the house – and for how long, above all? – a person of whom I was in ignorance. It lasted while I just bridled a little with the sense of how my office seemed to require that there should be no such ignorance and no such person. It lasted while this visitant, at all events – and there was a touch of the strange freedom, as I remember, in the sign of familiarity of his wearing no hat – seemed to fix me, from his position, with just the question, just the scrutiny through the fading light, that his own presence provoked. We were too far apart to call to each other, but there was a moment at which, at shorter range, some challenge between us, breaking the hush, would have been the right result of our straight mutual stare. He was in one of the angles, the one away from the house, very erect, as it struck me, and with both hands on the ledge. So I saw him as I see the letters I form on this page; then, exactly, after a minute, as if to add to the spectacle, he slowly changed his place – passed, looking at me hard all the while, to the opposite corner of the platform. Yes, it was intense to me that during this transit he never took his eyes from me, and I can see at this moment the way his hand as he went, moved from one of the crenellations to the next. He stopped at the other corner, but less long, and even as he turned away still markedly fixed me. He turned away; that was all I knew.

CHAPTER 4

It was not that I didn't wait, on this occasion, for more, since I was as deeply rooted as shaken. Was there a 'secret' at Bly – a mystery of Udolpho or an insane, an unmentionable relative kept in unsuspected confinement? I can't say how long I turned it over, or how long, in a confusion of curiosity and dread, I remained where I had had my collision; I only recall that when I re-entered the house, darkness had quite closed in. Agitation, in the interval, certainly had held me and driven me, for I must, in circling about the place, have walked three miles; but I was to be later on so much more overwhelmed that this mere dawn of alarm was a comparatively human chill. The most singular part of it, in fact – singular as the rest had been – was the part I became, in the hall, aware of in meeting Mrs Grose. This picture comes back to me in the general train – the impression, as I received it on my return, of the wide white panelled space, bright in the lamplight and with its portraits and red carpets, and of the good surprised look of my friend, which immediately told me she had missed me. It came to me straightaway, under her contact, that, with plain heartiness, mere relieved anxiety at my appearance, she knew nothing whatever that could bear upon the incident I had there ready for her. I had not suspected in advance that her comfortable face would pull me up, and I somehow measured the importance of what I had seen by my thus finding myself hesitate to mention it. Scarce anything in the whole history seems to me so odd as this fact that my real beginning of fear was one, as I may say, with the instinct of sparing my companion. On the spot, accordingly, in the pleasant hall and with her eyes on me, I, for a reason that I couldn't then have phrased, achieved an inward revolution – offered a vague pretext for my lateness and, with the plea of the beauty of the night and of the heavy dew and wet feet, went as soon as possible to my room.

Here it was another affair; here, for many days after, it was a queer affair enough. There were hours, from day to day – or at least there were moments, snatched even from clear duties – when I had to shut myself up to think. It wasn't so much yet that I was more nervous than I could bear to be as that I was remarkably afraid of becoming so; for the truth I had now to turn over was simply and clearly the truth that I could arrive at no account whatever of the visitor with whom I had been so inexplicably and yet, as it seemed to me, so intimately concerned. It took me little time to see that I might easily sound, without forms of inquiry and without exciting remark, any domestic complication. The shock I had suffered must have sharpened all my senses; I felt sure, at the end of three days and as the result of mere closer attention, that I had not been practised upon by the servants nor made the object of any 'game'. Of whatever it was that I knew, nothing was known around me. There was but one sane inference: some-one had taken a liberty rather monstrous. That was what, repeatedly, I dipped into my room and locked the door to say to myself. We had been, collectively, subject to an intrusion; some unscrupulous traveller, curious in old houses, had made his way in un-observed, enjoyed the prospect from the best point of view and then stolen out as he came. If he had given me such a bold, hard stare, that was but a part of his indiscretion. The good thing, after all, was that we should surely see no more of him.

This was not so good a thing, I admit, as not to leave me to judge that what, essentially, made nothing else much signify was simply my charming work. My charming work was just my life with Miles and Flora, and through nothing could I so like it as through feeling that to throw myself into it was to throw myself out of my trouble. The attraction of my small charges was a constant joy, leading me to wonder afresh at the vanity of my original fears, the distaste I had begun by entertaining for the probable grey prose of my office. There was to be no grey prose, it appeared, and no long grind; so how could work not be charming that presented itself as daily beauty? It was all the romance of the nursery and the poetry of the schoolroom. I don't mean by this, of course, that we studied only fiction and verse; I mean that I can express no otherwise the sort of interest my companions inspired. How can I describe that except by saying that instead of growing deadly used to them – and it's a marvel for a governess: I call the sisterhood to witness! – I made constant fresh discoveries. There was one direction, assuredly, in which these discoveries stopped: deep obscurity continued to cover the region of the boy's conduct at school. It had been promptly given me, I have noted, to face that mystery without a pang. Perhaps even it would be nearer the truth to say that – without a word – he himself had cleared it up. He had made the whole charge absurd. My conclusion bloomed there with the real rose-flush of his innocence: he was only too fine and fair for the little horrid, unclean school-world, and he had paid a price for it. I reflected acutely that the sense of such individual differences, such superiorities of quality, always, on the part of the majority – which could include even stupid sordid headmasters – turns infallibly to the vindictive.

Both the children had a gentleness – it was their only fault, and it never made Miles a muff – that kept them (how shall I express it?) almost impersonal and certainly quite unpunishable. They were like those cherubs of the anecdote who had – morally, at any rate – nothing to whack! I remember feeling with Miles especially as if he had had, as it were, nothing to call even an infinitesimal history. We expect of a small child scant enough 'antecedents', but there was in this beautiful little boy something extraordinarily sensitive, yet extraordinarily happy, that, more than in any creature of his age I have seen, struck me as beginning anew each day. He had never for a second suffered. I took this as a direct disproof of his having really been chastised. If he had been wicked he would have 'caught' it, and I should have caught it by the rebound – I should have found the trace, should have felt the wound and the dishonour. I could reconstitute nothing at all, and he was therefore an angel. He never spoke of his school, never mentioned a comrade or a master; and I, for my part, was quite too much disgusted to allude to them. Of course I was under the spell, and the wonderful part is that, even at the time, I perfectly knew I was. But I gave myself up to it; it was an antidote to any pain, and I had more pains than one. I was in receipt in these days of disturbing letters from home, where things were not going well. But with this joy of my children, what things in the world mattered? That was the question I used to put to my scrappy retirements. I was dazzled by their loveliness.

There was a Sunday – to get on – when it rained with such force and for so many hours that there could be no procession to church; in consequence of which, as the day declined, I had arranged with Mrs Grose that, should the evening show improvement, we would attend together the late service. The rain happily stopped, and I prepared for our walk, which, through the park and by the good road to the village, would be a matter of twenty minutes. Coming downstairs to meet my colleague in the hall, I remembered a pair of gloves that had required three stitches and that had received them – with a publicity perhaps not edifying – while I sat with the children at their tea, served on Sundays, by exception, in that cold clean temple of mahogany and brass, the 'grown-up' dining-room. The gloves had been dropped there, and I turned in to recover them. The day was grey enough, but the afternoon light still lingered, and it enabled me, on crossing the threshold, not only to recognise, on a chair near the wide window, then closed, the articles I wanted, but to become aware of a person on the other side of the window and looking straight in. One step into the room had sufficed; my vision was instantaneous; it was all there. The person looking straight in was the person who had already appeared to me. He appeared thus again with I won't say greater distinctness, for that was impossible, but with a nearness that represented a forward stride in our intercourse and made me, as I met him, catch my breath and turn cold. He was the same – he was the same, and seen, this time, as he had been seen before, from the waist up, the window, though the dining-room was on the ground floor, not going down to the terrace on which he stood. His face was close to the glass, yet the effect of this better view was, strangely, just to show me how intense the former had been. He remained but a few seconds – long enough to convince me he also saw and recognised; but it was as if I had been looking at him for years and had known him always. Something, however, happened this time that had not happened before; his stare into my face, through the glass and across the room, was as deep and hard as then, but it quitted me for a moment during which I could still watch it, see it fix successively several other things.

On the spot there came to me the added shock of a certitude that it was not for me he had come. He had come for someone else.

The flash of this knowledge – for it was knowledge in the midst of dread – produced in me the most extraordinary effect, starting, as I stood there, a sudden vibration of duty and courage. I say courage because I was beyond all doubt already far gone. I bounded straight out of the door again, reached that of the house, got in an instant upon the drive and, passing along the terrace as fast as I could rush, turned a corner and came full in sight. But it was in sight of nothing now – my visitor had vanished. I stopped, almost dropped, with the real relief of this; but I took in the whole scene – I gave him time to reappear. I call it time, but how long was it? I can't speak to the purpose today of the duration of these things. That kind of measure must have left me: they couldn't have lasted as they actually appeared to me to last. The terrace and the whole place, the lawn and the garden behind it, all I could see of the park, were empty with a great emptiness. There were shrubberies and big trees, but I remember the clear assurance I felt that none of them concealed him. He was there or was not there: not there if I didn't see him. I got hold of this; then, instinctively, instead of returning as I had come, went to the window. It was confusedly present to me that I ought to place myself where he had stood. I did so; I applied my face to the pane and looked, as he had looked, into the room. As if, at this moment, to show me exactly what his range had been, Mrs Grose, as I had done for himself just before, came in from the hall. With this I had the full image of a repetition of what had already occurred. She saw me as I had seen my own visitant; she pulled up short as I had done; I gave her something of the shock that I had received. She turned white, and this made me ask myself if I had blanched as much. She stared, in short, and retreated just on *my* lines, and I knew she had then passed out and come round to me and that I should presently meet her. I remained where I was, and while I waited I thought of more things than one. But there's only one I take space to mention. I wondered why *she* should be scared.

CHAPTER 5

Oh, she let me know as soon as, round the corner of the house, she loomed again into view. 'What in the name of goodness is the matter – ?' She was now flushed and out of breath.

I said nothing till she came quite near. 'With me?' I must have made a wonderful face. 'Do I show it?'

'You're as white as a sheet. You look awful.'

I considered; I could meet on this, without scruple – any degree of innocence. My need to respect the bloom of Mrs Grose's had dropped, without a rustle, from my shoulders, and if I wavered for the instant it was not with what I kept back. I put out my hand to her and she took it; I held her hard a little, liking to feel her close to me. There was a kind of support in the shy heave of her surprise. 'You came for me for church, of course, but I can't go.'

'Has anything happened?'

'Yes. You must know now. Did I look very queer?'

'Through this window? Dreadful!'

'Well,' I said, 'I've been frightened.' Mrs Grose's eyes expressed plainly that *she* had no wish to be, yet also that she knew too well her place not to be ready to share with me any marked inconvenience. Oh, it was quite settled that she *must* share! 'Just what you saw from the dining-room a minute ago was the effect of that. What *I* saw – just before – was much worse.'

Her hand tightened. 'What was it?'

'An extraordinary man. Looking in.'

'What extraordinary man?'

'I haven't the least idea.'

Mrs Grose gazed round us in vain. 'Then where is he gone?'

'I know still less.'

'Have you seen him before?'

'Yes – once. On the old tower.'

She could only look at me harder. 'Do you mean he's a stranger?'

'Oh, very much!'

'Yet you didn't tell me?'

'No – for reasons. But now that you've guessed – '

Mrs Grose's round eyes encountered this charge. 'Ah, I haven't guessed!' she said very simply. 'How can I if *you* don't imagine?'

'I don't in the very least.'

'You've seen him nowhere but on the tower?'

'And on this spot just now.'

Mrs Grose looked round again. 'What was he doing on the tower?'

'Only standing there and looking down at me.'

She thought a minute. 'Was he a gentleman?'

I found I had no need to think. 'No.' She gazed in deeper wonder. 'No.'

'Then nobody about the place? Nobody from the village?'

'Nobody – nobody. I didn't tell you, but I made sure.'

She breathed a vague relief: this was, oddly, so much to the good. It only went indeed a little way. 'But if he isn't a gentleman – '

'What *is* he? He's a horror.'

'A horror?'

'He's – God help me if I know *what* he is!'

Mrs Grose looked round once more; she fixed her eyes on the duskier distance and then, pulling herself together, turned to me with full inconsequence. 'It's time we should be at church.'

'Oh, I'm not fit for church!'

'Won't it do you good?'

'It won't do *them* – !' I nodded at the house.

'The children?'

'I can't leave them now.'

'You're afraid – ?'

I spoke boldly. 'I'm afraid of *him*.'

Mrs Grose's large face showed me, at this, for the first time, the faraway faint glimmer of a consciousness more acute: I somehow made out in it the delayed dawn of an idea I myself had not given her and that was as yet quite obscure to me. It comes back to me that I thought instantly of this as something I could get from her; and I felt it to be connected with the desire she presently showed to know more. 'When was it – on the tower?'

'About the middle of the month. At this same hour.'

'Almost at dark,' said Mrs Grose.

'Oh, no, not nearly. I saw him as I see you.'

'Then how did he get in?'

45

'And how did he get out?' I laughed. 'I had no opportunity to ask him! This evening, you see,' I pursued, 'he has not been able to get in.'

'He only peeps?'

'I hope it will be confined to that!' She had now let go my hand; she turned away a little. I waited an instant; then I brought out: 'Go to church. Goodbye. I must watch.'

Slowly she faced me again. 'Do you fear for them?'

We met in another long look. 'Don't *you*?' Instead of answering she came nearer to the window and, for a minute, applied her face to the glass. 'You see how he could see,' I meanwhile went on.

She didn't move. 'How long was he here?'

'Till I came out. I came to meet him.'

Mrs Grose at last turned round, and there was still more in her face: '*I* couldn't have come out.'

'Neither could I!' I laughed again. 'But I did come. I've my duty.'

'So have I mine,' she replied; after which she added: 'What's he like?'

'I've been dying to tell you. But he's like nobody.'

'Nobody?' she echoed.

'He has no hat.' Then seeing in her face that she already, in this, with a deeper dismay, found a touch of picture, I quickly added stroke to stroke. 'He has red hair, very red, close-curling, and a pale face, long in shape, with straight, good features and little, rather queer whiskers that are as red as his hair. His eyebrows are somehow darker; they look particularly arched and as if they might move a good deal. His eyes are sharp, strange – awfully; but I only know clearly that they're rather small and very fixed. His mouth's wide and his lips are thin, and except for his little whiskers he's quite clean-shaven. He gives me a sort of sense of looking like an actor.'

'An actor!' It was impossible to resemble one less, at least, than Mrs Grose at that moment.

'I've never seen one, but so I suppose them. He's tall, active, erect,' I continued, 'but never – no, never! – a gentleman.'

My companion's face had blanched as I went on; her round eyes started and her mild mouth gaped. 'A gentleman?' she gasped, confounded, stupefied: 'a gentleman *he*?'

'You know him then?'

She visibly tried to hold herself. 'But he *is* handsome?'

I saw the way to help her. 'Remarkably!'

'And dressed – ?'

'In somebody's clothes. They're smart, but they're not his own.'

She broke into a breathless affirmative groan. 'They're the master's!'

I caught it up. 'You *do* know him?'

She faltered but a second. 'Quint!' she cried.

'Quint?'

'Peter Quint – his own man, his valet, when he was here!'

'When the master was?'

Gaping still, but meeting me, she pieced it all together. 'He never wore his hat, but he did wear – well, there were waistcoats missed! They were both here – last year. Then the master went, and Quint was alone.'

I followed, but halting a little. 'Alone?'

'Alone with *us*.' Then as from a deeper depth, 'In charge,' she added.

47

'And what became of him?'

She hung fire so long that I was still more mystified. 'He went too,' she brought out at last.

'Went where?'

Her expression, at this, became extraordinary. 'God knows where! He died.'

'Died?' I almost shrieked.

She seemed fairly to square herself, plant herself more firmly to express the wonder of it. 'Yes. Mr Quint's dead.'

CHAPTER 6

It took of course more than that particular passage to place us together in presence of what we had now to live with as we could, my dreadful liability to impressions of the order so vividly exemplified, and my companion's knowledge henceforth – a know-ledge half consternation and half compassion – of that liability. There had been this evening, after the revelation that left me for an hour so prostrate – there had been for either of us no attendance on any service but a little service of tears and vows, of prayers and promises, a climax to the series of mutual challenges and pledges that had straightway ensued on our retreating together to the schoolroom and shutting ourselves up there to have everything out. The result of our having everything out was simply to reduce our situation to the last rigour of its elements. She herself had seen nothing, not the shadow of a shadow, and nobody in the house but the governess was in the governess's plight; yet she accepted without directly impugning my sanity the truth as I gave it to her, and ended by showing me on this ground an awestricken tenderness, a deference to my more than questionable privilege, of which the very breath has remained with me as that of the sweetest of human charities.

What was settled between us accordingly that night was that we thought we might bear things together; and I was not even sure that in spite of her exemption it was she who had the best of the burden. I knew at this hour, I think, as well as I knew later, what I was capable of meeting to shelter my pupils; but it took me some time to be wholly sure of what my honest comrade was prepared for to keep terms with so stiff an agreement. I was queer company enough – quite as queer as the company I received; but as I trace over what we went through, I see how much common ground we must have found in the one idea that, by good fortune, *could* steady us. It was the idea, the second movement, that led me straight out, as I may say, of the inner chamber of my dread. I could take the air in the court, at least, and there Mrs Grose could join me. Perfectly can I recall now the particular way strength came to me before we separated for the night. We had gone over and over every feature of what I had seen.

'He was looking for someone else, you say – someone who was not you?'

'He was looking for little Miles.' A portentous clearness now possessed me. '*That's* whom he was looking for.'

'But how do you know?'

'I know, I know, I know!' My exaltation grew. 'And *you* know, my dear!'

She didn't deny this, but I required, I felt, not even

so much telling as that. She took it up again in a moment. 'What if *he* should see him?'

'Little Miles? That's what he wants!'

She looked immensely scared again. 'The child?'

'Heaven forbid! The man. He wants to appear to *them*.' That he might was an awful conception, and yet somehow I could keep it at bay; which moreover, as we lingered there, was what I succeeded in practically proving. I had an absolute certainty that I should see again what I had already seen, but something within me said that by offering myself bravely as the sole subject of such experience, by accepting, by inviting, by surmounting it all, I should serve as an expiatory victim and guard the tranquillity of the rest of the household. The children especially I should thus fence about and absolutely save. I recall one of the last things I said that night to Mrs Grose.

'It does strike me that my pupils have never mentioned – !'

She looked at me hard as I musingly pulled up. 'His having been here and the time they were with him?'

'The time they were with him, and his name, his presence, his history, in any way. They've never alluded to it.'

'Oh, the little lady doesn't remember. She never heard or knew.'

'The circumstances of his death?' I thought with some intensity. 'Perhaps not. But Miles would remember – Miles would know.'

'Ah, don't try him!' broke from Mrs Grose.

I returned her the look she had given me. 'Don't be afraid.' I continued to think. 'It *is* rather odd.'

'That he has never spoken of him?'

'Never by the least reference. And you tell me they were "great friends"?'

'Oh, it wasn't *him*!' Mrs Grose with emphasis declared. 'It was Quint's own fancy. To play with him, I mean – to spoil him.' She paused a moment; then she added: 'Quint was much too free.'

This gave me, straight from my vision of his face – *such* a face! – a sudden sickness of disgust. 'Too free with *my* boy?'

'Too free with everyone!'

I forbore for the moment to analyse this description further than by the reflection that a part of it applied to several of the members of the household, of the half-dozen maids and men who were still of our small colony. But there was everything, for our apprehension, in the lucky fact that no discomfortable legend, no perturbation of scullions, had ever, within anyone's memory, attached to the kind old place. It had neither bad name nor ill fame, and Mrs Grose, most apparently, only desired to cling to me and to quake in silence. I even put her, the very last thing of all, to the test. It was when, at midnight, she had her hand on the schoolroom door to take leave. 'I *have* it from you, then – for it's of great importance – that he was definitely and admittedly bad?'

'Oh, not admittedly. I knew it – but the master didn't.'

'And you never told him?'

'Well, he didn't like tale bearing – he hated complaints. He was terribly short with anything of that kind, and if people were all right to *him* – '

'He wouldn't be bothered with more?' This squared well enough with my impression of him: he was not a trouble-loving gentleman, nor so very particular perhaps about some of the company he himself kept. All the same, I pressed my informant. 'I promise you, *I* would have told!'

She felt my discrimination. 'I dare say I was wrong. But really I was afraid.'

'Afraid of what?'

'Of things that man could do. Quint was so clever – he was so deep.'

I took this in still more than I probably showed. 'You weren't afraid of anything else? Not of his effect – ?'

'His effect?' she repeated with a face of anguish and waiting while I faltered.

'On innocent little precious lives. They were in your charge.'

'No, they weren't in mine!' she roundly and distressfully returned. 'The master believed in him and placed him here because he was supposed not to be quite in health and the country air so good for him. So he had everything to say. Yes' – she let me have it – 'even about *them*.'

'Them – that creature?' I had to smother a kind of howl. 'And you could bear it?'

'No. I couldn't – and I can't now!' And the poor woman burst into tears.

A rigid control, from the next day, was, as I have said, to follow them; yet how often and how passionately, for a week, we came back together to the subject! Much as we had discussed it that Sunday night, I was, in the immediate later hours especially – for it may be imagined whether I slept – still haunted with the shadow of something she had not told me. I myself had kept back nothing, but there was a word Mrs Grose had kept back. I was sure, moreover, by morning that this was not from a failure of frankness, but because on every side there were fears. It seems to me indeed, in raking it all over, that by the time the morrow's sun was high I had restlessly read into the facts before us almost all the meaning they were to receive from subsequent and more cruel occurrences. What they gave me, above all, was just the sinister figure of the living man – the dead one would keep awhile! – and of the months he had continuously passed at Bly, which, added up, made a formidable stretch. The limit of this evil time had arrived only when, on the dawn of a winter's morning, Peter Quint was found, by a labourer going to early work, stone dead on the road from the village: a catastrophe explained – superficially at least – by a visible wound to his head, such a wound as might have been produced (and as, on the final evidence, *had* been) by a fatal slip, in the dark and after leaving the public house, on the steepish icy slope, a wrong path altogether, at the bottom of which he lay. The icy slope, the turn mistaken at night and in liquor, accounted for much – practically, in the end and after the inquest and boundless chatter, for everything; but there had been matters in his life – strange passages and perils, secret disorders, vices more than suspected, that would have accounted for a good deal more.

I scarce know how to put my story into words that shall be a credible picture of my state of mind; but I was in these days literally able to find a joy in the extraordinary flight of heroism the occasion demanded of me. I now saw that I had been asked for a service admirable and difficult; and there would be a greatness in letting it be seen – oh, in the right quarter! – that I could succeed where many another

girl might have failed. It was an immense help to me –
I confess I rather applaud myself as I look back! – that
I saw my response so strongly and so simply. I was
there to protect and defend the little creatures in the
world the most bereaved and the most lovable, the
appeal of whose helplessness had suddenly become
only too explicit, a deep, constant ache of one's own
engaged affection. We were cut off, really, together;
we were united in our danger. They had nothing but
me, and I – well, I had them. It was, in short, a
magnificent chance. This chance presented itself to
me in an image richly material. I was a screen – I was
to stand before them. The more I saw, the less they
would. I began to watch them in a stifled suspense, a
disguised tension, that might well, had it continued
too long, have turned to something like madness.
What saved me, as I now see, was that it turned to
another matter altogether. It didn't last as suspense –
it was superseded by horrible proofs. Proofs, I say,
yes – from the moment I really took hold.

This moment dated from an afternoon hour that I
happened to spend in the grounds with the younger
of my pupils alone. We had left Miles indoors, on the
red cushion of a deep window-seat; he had wished to
finish a book, and I had been glad to encourage a
purpose so laudable in a young man whose only
defect was a certain ingenuity of restlessness. His
sister, on the contrary, had been alert to come out,
and I strolled with her half an hour, seeking the shade,
for the sun was still high and the day exceptionally
warm. I was aware afresh with her, as we went, of
how, like her brother, she contrived – it was the
charming thing in both children – to let me alone
without appearing to drop me and to accompany me

without appearing to oppress. They were never importunate and yet never listless. My attention to them all really went to seeing them amuse themselves immensely without me: this was a spectacle they seemed actively to prepare and that employed me as an active admirer. I walked in a world of their invention – they had no occasion whatever to draw upon mine; so that my time was taken only with being for them some remarkable person or thing that the game of the moment required and that was merely, thanks to my superior, my exalted stamp, a happy and highly distinguished sinecure. I forget what I was on the present occasion; I only remember that I was something very important and very quiet and that Flora was playing very hard. We were on the edge of the lake, and, as we had lately begun geography, the lake was the Sea of Azov.

Suddenly, amid these elements, I became aware that on the other side of the Sea of Azov we had an interested spectator. The way this knowledge gathered in me was the strangest thing in the world – the strangest, that is, except the very much stranger in which it quickly merged itself. I had sat down with a piece of work – for I was something or other that could sit – on the old stone bench which overlooked the pond; and in this position I began to take in with certitude and yet without direct vision the presence, a good way off, of a third person. The old trees, the thick shrubbery, made a great and pleasant shade, but it was all suffused with the brightness of the hot, still hour. There was no ambiguity in anything; none whatever, at least, in the conviction I from one moment to another found myself forming as to what I should see straight before me and across the lake as a consequence of raising my eyes. They were attached at this juncture to the stitching in which I was engaged, and I can feel once more the spasm of my effort not to move them till I should so have steadied myself as to be able to make up my mind what to do. There was an alien object in view – a figure whose right of presence I instantly and passionately questioned. I recollect counting over perfectly the possibilities, reminding myself that nothing was more natural, for instance, than the appearance of one of the men about the place, or even of a messenger, a postman or a tradesman's boy, from the village. That reminder had as little effect on my practical certitude as I was conscious – still even without looking – of its having upon the character and attitude of our visitor. Nothing was more natural than that these things should be the other things they absolutely were not.

Of the positive identity of the apparition I would assure myself as soon as the small clock of my courage should have ticked out the right second; meanwhile, with an effort that was already sharp enough, I transferred my eyes straight to little Flora, who, at the moment, was about ten yards away. My heart had stood still for an instant with the wonder and terror of the question whether she too would see; and I held my breath while I waited for what a cry from her, what some sudden innocent sign either of interest or of alarm, would tell me. I waited, but nothing came; then in the first place – and there is something more dire in this, I feel, than in anything I have to relate – I was determined by a sense that within a minute all spontaneous sounds from her had dropped; and in the second by the circumstance that also within the minute she had, in her play, turned her back to the water. This was her attitude when I at last looked at her – looked with the confirmed conviction that we were still, together, under direct personal notice. She had picked up a small, flat piece of wood which happened to have in it a little hole that had evidently suggested to her the idea of sticking in another fragment that might figure as a mast and make the thing a boat. This second morsel, as I watched her, she was very markedly and intently attempting to tighten in its place. My apprehension of what she was doing sustained me so that after some seconds I felt I was ready for more. Then I again shifted my eyes – I faced what I had to face.

CHAPTER 7

I got hold of Mrs Grose as soon after this as I could; and I can give no intelligible account of how I fought out the interval. Yet I still hear myself cry as I fairly threw myself into her arms: 'They *know* – it's too monstrous: they know, they know!'

'And what on earth – ?' I felt her incredulity as she held me.

'Why, all that *we* know – and heaven knows what more besides!' Then as she released me I made it out to her, made it out perhaps only now with full coherency even to myself. 'Two hours ago, in the garden' – I could scarce articulate – 'Flora *saw*!'

Mrs Grose took it as she might have taken a blow in the stomach. 'She has told you?' she panted.

'Not a word – that's the horror. She kept it to herself! The child of eight, *that* child!' Unutterable still for me was the stupefaction of it.

Mrs Grose of course could only gape the wider. 'Then how do you know?'

'I was there – I saw with my eyes: saw she was perfectly aware.'

'Do you mean aware of *him*?'

'No – of *her*.' I was conscious as I spoke that I looked prodigious things, for I got the slow reflection of them in my companion's face. 'Another person – this time; but a figure of quite as unmistakable horror and evil: a woman in black, pale and dreadful – with such an air also, and such a face! – on the other side of the lake. I was there with the child – quiet for the hour; and in the midst of it she came.'

'Came how – from where?'

'From where they come from! She just appeared and stood there – but not so near.'

'And without coming nearer?'

'Oh, for the effect and the feeling she might have been as close as you!'

My friend, with an odd impulse, fell back a step. 'Was she someone you've never seen?'

'Never. But someone the child has. Someone *you* have.' Then to show how I had thought it all out: 'My predecessor – the one who died.'

'Miss Jessel?'

'Miss Jessel. You don't believe me?' I pressed.

She turned right and left in her distress. 'How can you be sure?'

This drew from me, in the state of my nerves, a flash of impatience. 'Then ask Flora – she's sure!' But I had no sooner spoken than I caught myself up. 'No, for God's sake, *don't*. She'll say she isn't – she'll lie!'

Mrs Grose was not too bewildered instinctively to protest. 'Ah, how *can* you?'

'Because I'm clear. Flora doesn't want me to know.'

'It's only then to spare you.'

'No, no – there are depths, depths! The more I go over it the more I see in it, and the more I see in it the more I fear. I don't know what I *don't* see – what I *don't* fear!'

Mrs Grose tried to keep up with me. 'You mean you're afraid of seeing her again?'

'Oh, no; that's nothing – now!' Then I explained. 'It's of *not* seeing her.'

But my companion only looked wan. 'I don't understand.'

'Why, it's that the child may keep it up – and that the child assuredly *will* – without my knowing it.'

At the image of this possibility Mrs Grose for a moment collapsed, yet presently pulled herself together again as if from the positive force of the sense of what, should we yield an inch, there would really be to give way to. 'Dear, dear – we must keep our heads! And after all, if she doesn't mind it – !' She even tried a grim joke. 'Perhaps she likes it!'

'Likes *such* things – a scrap of an infant!'

'Isn't it just a proof of her blest innocence?' my friend bravely inquired.

She brought me, for the instant, almost round. 'Oh, we must clutch at that – we must cling to it! If it isn't a proof of what you say, it's a proof of – God knows what! For the woman's a horror of horrors.'

Mrs Grose, at this, fixed her eyes a minute on the ground; then at last raising them, 'Tell me how you know,' she said.

'Then you admit it's what she was?' I cried.

'Tell me how you know,' my friend simply repeated.

'Know? By seeing her! By the way she looked.'

'At you, do you mean – so wickedly?'

'Dear me, no – I could have borne that. She gave me never a glance. She only fixed the child.'

Mrs Grose tried to see it. 'Fixed her?'

'Ah, with such awful eyes!'

She stared at mine as if they might really have resembled them. 'Do you mean of dislike?'

'God help us, no. Of something much worse.'

'Worse than dislike?' – this left her indeed at a loss.

'With a determination – indescribable. With a kind of fury of intention.'

I made her turn pale. 'Intention?'

'To get hold of her.' Mrs Grose – her eyes just lingering on mine – gave a shudder and walked to the window; and while she stood there looking out I completed my statement. '*That's* what Flora knows.'

After a little she turned round. 'The person was in black, you say?'

'In mourning – rather poor, almost shabby. But – yes – with extraordinary beauty.' I now recognised to what I had at last, stroke by stroke, brought the victim of my confidence, for she quite visibly weighed this. 'Oh, handsome – very, very,' I insisted; 'wonderfully handsome. But infamous.'

She slowly came back to me. 'Miss Jessel – *was* infamous.' She once more took my hand in both her own, holding it as tight as if to fortify me against the increase of alarm I might draw from this disclosure. 'They were both infamous,' she finally said.

So for a little we faced it once more together; and I found absolutely a degree of help in seeing it now so straight. 'I appreciate,' I said, 'the great decency of your not having hitherto spoken; but the time has certainly come to give me the whole thing.' She appeared to assent to this, but still only in silence; seeing which I went on: 'I must have it now. Of what did she die? Come, there was something between them.'

'There was everything.'

'In spite of the difference – ?'

'Oh, of their rank, their condition' – she brought it woefully out. '*She* was a lady.'

I turned it over; I again saw. 'Yes – she was a lady.'

'And he so dreadfully below,' said Mrs Grose.

I felt that I doubtless needn't press too hard, in such company, on the place of a servant in the scale; but there was nothing to prevent an acceptance of my companion's own measure of my predecessor's abasement. There was a way to deal with that, and I dealt; the more readily for my full vision – on the evidence – of our employer's late good-looking 'own' man; impudent, assured, spoiled, depraved. 'The fellow was a hound.'

Mrs Grose considered as if it were perhaps a little a case for a sense of shades. 'I've never seen one like him. He did what he wished.'

'With *her*?'

'With them all.'

It was as if now in my friend's own eyes Miss Jessel had again appeared. I seemed at any rate for an instant to trace their evocation of her as distinctly as I had seen her by the pond; and I brought out with decision: 'It must have been also what *she* wished!'

Mrs Grose's face signified that it had been indeed, but she said at the same time: 'Poor woman – she paid for it!'

'Then you do know what she died of?' I asked.

'No – I know nothing. I wanted not to know; I was

glad enough I didn't – and I thanked heaven she was well out of this!'

'Yet you had then your idea – '

'Of her real reason for leaving? Oh, yes – as to that. She couldn't have stayed. Fancy it here – for a governess! And afterwards I imagined – and I still imagine. And what I imagine is dreadful.'

'Not so dreadful as what *I* do,' I replied; on which I must have shown her – as I was indeed but too conscious – a front of miserable defeat. It brought out again all her compassion for me, and at the renewed touch of her kindness, my power to resist broke down. I burst, as I had the other time made her burst, into tears; she took me to her motherly breast, and my lamentation overflowed. 'I don't do it!' I sobbed in despair. 'I don't save or shield them! It's far worse than I dreamed. They're lost!'

CHAPTER 8

What I had said to Mrs Grose was true enough. There were in the matter I had put before her depths and possibilities that I lacked resolution to sound, so that when we met once more in the wonder of it, we were of a common mind about the duty of resistance to extravagant fancies. We were to keep our heads if we should keep nothing else – difficult indeed as that might be in the face of all that, in our prodigious experience, seemed least to be questioned. Late that night, while the house slept, we had another talk in my room; when she went all the way with me as to its being beyond doubt that I had seen exactly what I had seen. I found that to keep her thoroughly in the grip of this I had only to ask her how, if I had 'made it up', I came to be able to give, of each of the persons appearing to me, a picture disclosing, to the last detail, their special marks – a portrait on the exhibition of which she had instantly recognised and named them. She wished, of course – small blame to her! – to sink the whole subject; and I was quick to assure her that my own interest in it had now violently taken the form of a search for the way to escape from it. I closed with her cordially on the article of the likelihood that with recurrence – for recurrence we took for granted – I should get used to my danger; distinctly professing that my personal exposure had suddenly become the least of my discomforts. It was my new suspicion that was intolerable; and yet even to this complication the later hours of the day had brought a little ease.

On leaving her, after my first outbreak, I had of course returned to my pupils, associating the right remedy for my dismay with that sense of their charm which I had already recognised as a resource I could positively cultivate and which had never failed me yet. I had simply, in other words, plunged afresh into Flora's special society and there become aware – it was almost a luxury! – that she could put her little conscious hand straight upon the spot that ached. She had looked at me in sweet speculation and then had accused me to my face of having 'cried'. I had supposed the ugly signs of it brushed away; but I could literally – for the time, at all events – rejoice, under this fathomless charity, that they had not entirely disappeared. To gaze into the depths of blue of the child's eyes and pronounce their loveliness a trick of premature cunning was to be guilty of a cynicism in preference to which I naturally preferred to abjure my judgement and, so far as might be, my agitation. I couldn't abjure for merely wanting to, but I could repeat to Mrs Grose – as I did there, over and over, in the small hours – that with our small friends, voices in the air, their pressure on one's heart and their fragrant faces against one's cheek, everything fell to the ground but their incapacity and their beauty. It was a pity that, somehow, to settle this once for all, I had equally to re-enumerate the signs of subtlety that, in the afternoon, by the lake, had made a miracle of my show of self-possession. It was a pity to be obliged to reinvestigate the certitude of the moment itself and repeat how it had come to me as a revelation that the inconceivable communion I then surprised must have been for both parties a matter of habit. It was a pity I should have had to quaver out again, the reasons for my not having, in my delusion, so much as questioned that the little girl saw our visitant even as I actually saw Mrs Grose herself, and that she wanted, by just so much as she did thus see, to make me suppose she didn't, and at the same time, without showing anything, arrive at a guess as to whether I myself did! It was a pity I needed to recapitulate the portentous little activities by which she sought to divert my attention – the perceptible increase of movement, the greater intensity of play, the singing, the gabbling of nonsense and the invitation to romp.

Yet if I had not indulged, to prove there was nothing in it, in this review, I should have missed the two or three dim elements of comfort that still remained to me. I shouldn't, for instance, have been able to asseverate to my friend that I was certain –

which was so much to the good – that *I* at least had not betrayed myself. I shouldn't have been prompted, by stress of need, by desperation of mind – I scarce know what to call it – to invoke such further aid to intelligence as might spring from pushing my colleague fairly to the wall. She had told me, bit by bit, under pressure, a great deal; but a small shifty spot on the wrong side of it all still sometimes brushed my brow like the wing of a bat; and I remember how on this occasion – for the sleeping house and the concentration alike of our danger and our watch seemed to help – I felt the importance of giving the last jerk to the curtain. 'I don't believe anything so horrible,' I recollect saying; 'no, let us put it definitely, my dear, that I don't. But if I did, you know, there's a thing I should require now, just without sparing you the least bit more – oh, not a scrap, come! – to get out of you. What was it you had in mind when, in our distress, before Miles came back, over the letter from his school, you said, under my insistence, that you didn't pretend for him he hadn't literally *ever* been "bad"? He has *not*, truly, "ever", in these weeks that I myself have lived with him and so closely watched him; he has been an imperturbable little prodigy of delightful, lovable goodness. Therefore you might perfectly have made the claim for him if you had not, as it happened, seen an exception to take. What was your exception, and to what passage in your personal observation of him did you refer?'

It was a straight question enough, but levity was not our note, and in any case I had, before the grey dawn admonished us to separate, got my answer. What my friend had had in mind proved immensely to the purpose. It was neither more nor less than the particular fact that for a period of several months Quint and the boy had been perpetually together. It was, indeed, the very appropriate item of evidence of her having ventured to criticise the propriety, to hint at the incongruity, of so close an alliance, and even to go so far on the subject as a frank overture to Miss Jessel would take her. Miss Jessel had, with a very high manner about it, requested her to mind her business, and the good woman had on this directly approached little Miles. What she had said to him, since I pressed, was that *she* liked to see young gentlemen not forget their station.

I pressed again, of course, the closer for that. 'You reminded him that Quint was only a base menial?'

'As you might say! And it was his answer, for one thing, that was bad.'

'And for another thing?' I waited. 'He repeated your words to Quint?'

'No, not that. It's just what he *wouldn't*!' she could still impress on me. 'I was sure, at any rate,' she added, 'that he didn't. But he denied certain occasions.'

'What occasions?'

'When they had been about together quite as if Quint were his tutor – and a very grand one – and Miss Jessel only for the little lady. When he had gone off with the fellow, I mean, and spent hours with him.'

'He then prevaricated about it – he said he hadn't?' Her assent was clear enough to cause me to add in a moment: 'I see. He lied.'

'Oh!' Mrs Grose mumbled. This was a suggestion that it didn't matter; which indeed she backed up by a further remark. 'You see, after all, Miss Jessel didn't mind. She didn't forbid him.'

I considered. 'Did he put that to you as a justification?'

At this she dropped again. 'No, he never spoke of it.'

'Never mentioned her in connection with Quint?'

She saw, visibly flushing, where I was coming out. 'Well, he didn't show anything. He denied,' she repeated; 'he denied.'

Lord, how I pressed her now! 'So that you could see he knew what was between the two wretches?'

'I don't know – I don't know!' the poor woman wailed.

'You do know, you dear thing,' I replied; 'only you haven't my dreadful boldness of mind, and you keep back, out of timidity, and modesty and delicacy, even the impression that in the past, when you had, without my aid, to flounder about in silence, most of all made you miserable. But I shall get it out of you yet! There was something in the boy that suggested to you,' I continued, 'his covering and concealing their relation.'

'Oh, he couldn't prevent – '

'Your learning the truth? I dare say! But, heavens,' I fell, with vehemence, a-thinking, 'what it shows that they must, to that extent, have succeeded in making of him!'

'Ah, nothing that's not nice *now*!' Mrs Grose lugubriously pleaded.

'I don't wonder you looked queer,' I persisted, 'when I mentioned to you the letter from his school!'

'I doubt if I looked as queer as you!' she retorted with homely force. 'And if he was so bad then as that comes to, how is he such an angel now?'

'Yes, indeed – and if he was a fiend at school! How,

67

how, how? Well,' I said in my torment, 'you must put it to me again, though I shall not be able to tell you for some days. Only put it to me again!' I cried in a way that made my friend stare. 'There are directions in which I mustn't for the present let myself go.' Meanwhile I returned to her first example – the one to which she had just previously referred – of the boy's happy capacity for an occasional slip. 'If Quint – on your remonstrance at the time you speak of – was a base menial, one of the things Miles said to you, I find myself guessing, was that you were another.' Again her admission was so adequate that I continued: 'And you forgave him that?'

'Wouldn't *you*?'

'Oh, yes!' And we exchanged there, in the stillness, a sound of the oddest amusement. Then I went on: 'At all events, while he was with the man – '

'Miss Flora was with the woman. It suited them all!'

It suited me too, I felt, only too well; by which I mean that it suited exactly the particular deadly view I was in the very act of forbidding myself to entertain. But I so far succeeded in checking the expression of this view that I will throw, just here, no further light on it than may be offered by the mention of my final observation to Mrs Grose. 'His having lied and been impudent are, I confess, less engaging specimens than I had hoped to have from you of the outbreak in him of the little natural man. Still,' I mused, 'they must do, for they make me feel more than ever that I must watch.'

It made me blush, the next minute, to see in my friend's face how much more unreservedly she had forgiven him than her anecdote struck me as pointing out to my own tenderness any way to do. This was marked when, at the schoolroom door, she quitted me. 'Surely you don't accuse *him* – '

'Of carrying on an intercourse that he conceals from me? Ah, remember that, until further evidence, I now accuse nobody.' Then before shutting her out to go by another passage to her own place, 'I must just wait,' I wound up.

CHAPTER 9

I waited and waited, and the days took as they elapsed something from my consternation. A very few of them, in fact, passing, in constant sight of my pupils, without a fresh incident, sufficed to give to grievous fancies and even to odious memories a kind of brush of the sponge. I have spoken of the surrender to their extraordinary childish grace as a thing I could actively promote in myself, and it may be imagined if I neglected now to apply at this source for whatever balm it would yield. Stranger than I can express, certainly, was the effort to struggle against my new lights. It would doubtless have been a greater tension still, however, had it not been so frequently successful. I used to wonder how my little charges could help guessing that I thought strange things about them; and the circumstance that these things only made them more interesting was not by itself a direct aid to keeping them in the dark. I trembled lest they should see that they *were* so immensely more interesting. Putting things at the worst, at all events, as in meditation I so often did, any clouding of their innocence could only be – blameless and foredoomed as they were – a reason the more for taking risks. There were moments when I knew myself to catch them up by an irresistible impulse and press them to my heart. As soon as I had done so, I used to wonder: 'What will they think of that? Doesn't it betray too much?' It would have been easy to get into a sad wild tangle about how much I might betray; but the real account, I feel, of the hours of peace I could still enjoy was that the immediate charm of my companions was a beguilement still effective even under the shadow of the possibility that it was studied. For if it occurred to me that I might occasionally excite suspicion by the little outbreaks of my sharper passion for them, so too I remember asking if I mightn't see a queerness in the traceable increase of their own demonstrations.

They were at this period extravagantly and preternaturally fond of me; which, after all, I could reflect was no more than a graceful response in children perpetually bowed down over and hugged. The homage of which they were so lavish succeeded in truth for my nerves quite as well as if I never appeared to myself, as I may say, literally to catch them at a purpose in it. They had never, I think, wanted to do so many things for their poor protectress; I mean – though they got their lessons better and better, which was naturally what would please her most – in the way of diverting, entertaining, surprising her; reading her passages, telling her stories, acting her charades, pouncing out at her in disguises, as animals and historical characters and above all, astonishing her by the 'pieces' they had secretly got by heart and could interminably recite. I should never get to the bottom – were I to let myself go even now – of the prodigious

private commentary, all under still more private cor-
rection, with which I in these days overscored their
full hours. They had shown me from the first a facility
for everything, a general faculty which, taking a fresh
start, achieved remarkable flights. They got their little
tasks as if they loved them; they indulged, from the
mere exuberance of the gift, in the most unimposed
little miracles of memory. They not only popped out
at me as tigers and as Romans, but as Shakespearians,
astronomers, and navigators. This was so singularly
the case that it had presumably much to do with the
fact as to which, at the present day, I am at a loss for
a different explanation: I allude to my unnatural com-
posure on the subject of another school for Miles.
What I remember is that I was content for the time
not to open the question, and that contentment must
have sprung from the sense of his perpetually striking
show of cleverness. He was too clever for a bad governess, for a parson's daughter, to spoil; and the
strangest if not the brightest thread in the pensive
embroidery I just spoke of was the impression I might
have got, if I had dared to work it out, that he was
under some influence operating in his small intellectual
life as a tremendous incitement.

If it was easy to reflect, however, that such a boy
could postpone school, it was at least as marked that
for such a boy to have been 'kicked out' by a school-
master was a mystification without end. Let me add
that in their company now – and I was careful almost
never to be out of it – I could follow no scent very far.
We lived in a cloud of music and affection and success
and private theatricals. The musical sense in each
of the children was of the quickest, but the elder
especially had a marvellous knack of catching and

repeating. The schoolroom piano broke into all gruesome fancies; and when that failed there were
confabulations in corners, with a sequel of one of
them going out in the highest spirits in order to 'come
in' as something new. I had had brothers myself, and
it was no revelation to me that little girls could be
slavish idolaters of little boys. What surpassed
everything was that there was a little boy in the world
who could have for the inferior age, sex, and
intelligence so fine a consideration. They were
extraordinarily at one, and to say that they never
either quarrelled or complained is to make the note of
praise coarse for their quality of sweetness. Sometimes
perhaps indeed (when I dropped into coarseness) I
came across traces of little understandings between
them by which one of them should keep me occupied
while the other slipped away. There is a naïf side, I
suppose, in all diplomacy; but if my pupils practised
upon me it was surely with the minimum of grossness.
It was all in the other quarter that, after a lull, the
grossness broke out.

I find that I really hang back; but I must take my
horrid plunge. In going on with the record of what
was hideous at Bly I not only challenge the most
liberal faith – for which I little care; but (and this is
another matter) I renew what I myself suffered, I
again push my dreadful way through it to the end.
There came suddenly an hour after which, as I look
back, the business seems to me to have been all pure
suffering; but I have at least reached the heart of it,
and the straightest road out is doubtless to advance.
One evening – with nothing to lead up or prepare it –
I felt the cold touch of the impression that had
breathed on me the night of my arrival and which,

much lighter then as I have mentioned, I should probably have made little of in memory had my sub-sequent sojourn been less agitated. I had not gone to bed; I sat reading by a couple of candles. There was a roomful of old books at Bly – last-century fiction some of it, which, to the extent of a distinctly deprecated renown, but never to so much as that of a stray specimen, had reached the sequestered home and appealed to the unavowed curiosity of my youth. I remember that the book I had in my hand was Fielding's *Amelia*; also that I was wholly awake. I recall further both a general conviction that it was horribly late and a particular objection to looking at my watch. I figure finally that the white curtain draping, in the fashion of those days, the head of Flora's little bed, shrouded, as I had assured myself long before, the perfection of childish rest. I recollect in short that though I was deeply interested in my author, I found myself, at the turn of a page and with his spell all scattered, looking straight up from him and hard at the door of my room. There was a moment during which I listened, reminded of the faint sense I had had, the first night, of there being something undefinably astir in the house, and noted the soft breath of the open casement just move the half-drawn blind. Then, with all the marks of a deliberation that must have seemed magnificent had there been anyone to admire it, I laid down my book, rose to my feet and, taking a candle, went straight out of the room and, from the passage, on which my light made little impression, noiselessly closed and locked the door.

I can say now neither what determined nor what guided me, but I went straight along the lobby, holding my candle high, till I came within sight of

the tall window that presided over the great turn
of the staircase. At this point, I precipitately found
myself aware of three things. They were practically
simultaneous, yet they had flashes of succession.
My candle, under a bold flourish, went out, and I
perceived, by the uncovered window, that the yielding
dusk of earliest morning rendered it unnecessary.
Without it, the next instant, I knew that there was
a figure on the stair. I speak of sequences, but I
required no lapse of seconds to stiffen myself for
a third encounter with Quint. The apparition had
reached the landing halfway up and was therefore on
the spot nearest the window, where, at sight of me, it
stopped short and fixed me exactly as it had fixed me
from the tower and from the garden. He knew me as
well as I knew him; and so, in the cold faint twilight,
with a glimmer in the high glass and another on the
polish of the oak stair below, we faced each other in
our common intensity. He was absolutely, on this
occasion, a living, detestable, dangerous presence.
But that was not the wonder of wonders; I reserve
this distinction for quite another circumstance: the
circumstance that dread had unmistakably quitted
me and that there was nothing in me unable to meet
and measure him.

I had plenty of anguish after that extraordinary
moment, but I had, thank God, no terror. And he
knew I hadn't – I found myself at the end of an
instant magnificently aware of this. I felt, in a fierce
rigour of confidence, that if I stood my ground a
minute I should cease – for the time at least – to
have him to reckon with; and during the minute,
accordingly, the thing was as human and hideous as
a real interview: hideous just because it *was* human,

74

as human as to have met alone, in the small hours, in a sleeping house, some enemy, some adventurer, some criminal. It was the dead silence of our long gaze at such close quarters that gave the whole horror, huge as it was, its only note of the unnatural. If I had met a murderer in such a place and at such an hour we still at least would have spoken. Something would have passed, in life, between us; if nothing had passed, one of us would have moved. The moment was so prolonged that it would have taken but little more to make me doubt if even *I* were in life. I can't express what followed it save by saying that the silence itself – which was indeed in a manner an attestation of my strength – became the element into which I saw the figure disappear; in which I definitely saw it turn, as I might have seen the low wretch to which it had once belonged turn on receipt of an order, and pass, with my eyes on the villainous back that no hunch could have more disfigured, straight down the staircase and into the darkness in which the next bend was lost.

CHAPTER 10

I remained awhile at the top of the stair, but with the effect presently of understanding that when my visitor had gone, he had gone; then I returned to my room. The foremost thing I saw there by the light of the candle I had left burning was that Flora's little bed was empty; and on this I caught my breath with all the terror that, five minutes before, I had been able to resist. I dashed at the place in which I had left her lying and over which – for the small silk counterpane and the sheets were disarranged – the white curtains had been deceivingly pulled forward; then my step, to my unutterable relief, produced an answering sound: I noticed an agitation of the window-blind, and the child, ducking down, emerged rosily from the other side of it. She stood there in so much of her candour and so little of her nightgown, with her pink bare feet and the golden glow of her curls. She looked intensely grave and I had never had such a sense of losing an advantage acquired (the thrill of which had just been so prodigious) as on my consciousness that she addressed me with a reproach: 'You naughty: where *have* you been?' Instead of challenging her own irregularity, I found myself arraigned and explaining. She herself explained, for that matter, with the loveliest, eagerest simplicity. She had known suddenly, as she lay there, that I was out of the room and had jumped up to see what had become of me. I had dropped, with the joy of her reappearance, back into my chair – feeling then, and then only, a little faint; and she had pattered straight over to me, thrown herself upon my knee, given herself to be held with the flame of the candle full in the wonderful little face that was still flushed with sleep. I remember closing my eyes an instant, yieldingly, consciously, as before the excess of something beautiful that shone out of the blue of her own. 'You were looking for me out of the window?' I said. 'You thought I might be walking in the grounds?'

'Well, you know, I thought someone was' – she never blanched as she smiled out that at me.

Oh, how I looked at her now! 'And did you see anyone?'

'Ah, *no*!' she returned almost (with the full privilege

76

of childish inconsequence) resentfully, though with a long sweetness in her little drawl of the negative.

At the moment, in the state of my nerves, I absolutely believed she lied, and if I once more closed my eyes it was before the dazzle of the three or four possible ways in which I might take this up. One of these for a moment tempted me with such singular force that, to resist it, I must have gripped my little girl with a spasm that, wonderfully, she submitted to without a cry or a sign of fright. Why not break out at her on the spot and have it all over? – give it to her straight in her lovely little lighted face? 'You see, you see, you *know* that you do and that you already quite suspect I believe it; therefore why not frankly confess it to me, so that we may at least live with it together and learn perhaps, in the strangeness of our fate, where we are and what it means?' This solicitation dropped, alas, as it came: if I could immediately have succumbed to it I might have spared myself – well, you'll see what. Instead of succumbing, I sprang again to my feet, looked at her bed and took a helpless middle way. 'Why did you pull the curtain over the place to make me think you were still there?'

Flora luminously considered; after which, with her little divine smile: 'Because I don't like to frighten you!'

'But if I had, by your idea, gone out – ?'

She absolutely declined to be puzzled; she turned her eyes to the flame of the candle as if the question were as irrelevant, or at any rate as impersonal, as Mrs Marcet or nine-times-nine. 'Oh, but you know,' she quite adequately answered, 'that you might come back, you dear, and that you *have*!' And after a little, when she had got into bed, I had, for a long time, by almost sitting on her for the retention of her hand, to show how I recognised the pertinence of my return.

You may imagine the general complexion, from that moment, of my nights. I repeatedly sat up till I didn't know when; I selected moments when my room-mate unmistakably slept, and, stealing out, took noiseless turns in the passage. I even pushed as far as to where I had last met Quint. But I never met him there again, and I may as well say at once that I on no other occasion saw him in the house. I just missed, on the staircase, nevertheless, a different adventure. Looking down it from the top I once recognised the presence of a woman seated on one of the lower steps with her back presented to me, her body half-bowed and her head, in an attitude of woe, in her hands. I had been there but an instant, however, when she vanished without looking round at me. I knew, for all that, exactly what dreadful face she had to show; and I wondered whether, if instead of being above I had been below, I should have had the same nerve for going up that I had lately shown Quint. Well, there continued to be plenty of call for nerve. On the eleventh night after my latest encounter with that gentleman – they were all numbered now – I had an alarm that perilously skirted it and that indeed, from the particular quality of its unexpectedness, proved quite my sharpest shock. It was precisely the first night during this series, that, weary with vigils, I had conceived I might again without laxity lay myself down at my old hour. I slept immediately and, as I afterwards knew, till about one o'clock; but when I woke it was to sit straight up as completely roused as if a hand had shaken me. I had left a light burning, but it was now out, and I felt an instant certainty that Flora had extinguished it. This brought me to my feet and straight, in the darkness, to her bed, which I found she had left. A glance at the window enlightened me further, and the striking of a match completed the picture.

The child had again got up – this time blowing out the taper, and had again, for some purpose of observation or response, squeezed in behind the blind and was peering out into the night. That she now saw as she had not, I had satisfied myself, the previous time – was proved to me by the fact that she was disturbed neither by my re-illumination nor by the haste I made to get into slippers and into a wrap. Hidden, protected, absorbed, she evidently rested on the sill – the casement opened forward – and gave herself up. There was a great still moon to help her, and this fact had counted in my quick decision. She was face to face with the apparition we had met at the lake, and could now communicate with it as she had not then been able to do. What I, on my side, had to care for was, without disturbing her, to reach, from the corridor, some other window turned to the same quarter. I got to the door without her hearing me; I got out of it, closed it, and listened from the other side for some sound from her. While I stood in the passage I had my eyes on her brother's door, which was but ten steps off and which, indescribably, produced in me a renewal of the strange impulse that I lately spoke of as my temptation. What if I should go straight in and march to *his* window? – what if, by risking to his boyish bewilderment a revelation of my motive, I should throw across the rest of the mystery the long halter of my boldness?

This thought held me sufficiently to make me cross to his threshold and pause again. I preternaturally listened; I figured to myself what might portentously be; I wondered if his bed were also empty and he also secretly at watch. It was a deep soundless minute, at the end of which my impulse failed. He was quiet; he might be innocent; the risk was hideous; I turned away. There was a figure in the grounds – a figure prowling for a sight, the visitor with whom Flora was engaged; but it wasn't the visitor most concerned with my boy. I hesitated afresh, but on other grounds and only a few seconds; then I had made my choice. There were empty rooms enough at Bly, and it was only a question of choosing the right one. The right one suddenly presented itself to me as the lower one – though high above the gardens – in the solid corner of the house that I have spoken of as the old tower. This was a large, square chamber, arranged with some state as a bedroom, the extravagant size of which made it so inconvenient that it had not for years, though kept by Mrs Grose in exemplary order, been occupied. I had often admired it and I knew my way about in it; I had only, after just faltering at the first chill gloom of its disuse, to pass across it and unbolt in all quietness one of the shutters. Achieving this transit I uncovered the glass without a sound and, applying my face to the pane, was able, the darkness without being much less than within, to see that I commanded the right direction. Then I saw something more. The moon made the night extraordinarily penetrable and showed me on the lawn a person, diminished by distance, who stood there motionless and as if fascinated, looking up to where I had appeared looking, that is, not so much straight at me as at something that was apparently above me. There was clearly another person above me – there was a person on the tower;

but the presence on the lawn was not in the least what I had conceived and had confidently hurried to meet. The presence on the lawn – I felt sick as I made it out – was poor little Miles himself.

CHAPTER II

It was not till late next day that I spoke to Mrs Grose; the rigour with which I kept my pupils in sight making it often difficult to meet her privately; the more as we each felt the importance of not provoking – on the part of the servants quite as much as on that of the children – any suspicion of a secret flurry or of a discussion of mysteries. I drew a great security in this particular from her mere smooth aspect. There was nothing in her fresh face to pass on to others the least of my horrible confidences. She believed me, I was sure, absolutely: if she hadn't I don't know what would have become of me, for I couldn't have borne the strain alone. But she was a magnificent monument to the blessing of a want of imagination, and if she could see in our little charges nothing but their beauty and amiability, their happiness and cleverness, she had no direct communication with the sources of my trouble. If they had been at all visibly blighted or battered, she would doubtless have grown, on tracing it back, haggard enough to match them; as matters stood, however, I could feel her, when she surveyed them with her large white arms folded and the habit of serenity in all her look, thank the Lord's mercy that if they were ruined the pieces would still serve. Flights of fancy gave place, in her mind, to a steady fireside glow, and I had already begun to perceive how, with the development of the conviction that – as time went on without a public accident – our young things could, after all, look out for themselves, she addressed her greatest solicitude to the sad case presented by their deputy-guardian. That, for myself, was a sound simplification: I could engage that, to the world, my face should tell no tales, but it would have been, in the conditions, an immense added worry to find myself anxious about hers.

At the hour I now speak of she had joined me, under pressure, on the terrace, where, with the lapse of the season, the afternoon sun was now agreeable; and we sat there together while before us and at a distance, yet within call if we wished, the children strolled to and fro in one of their most manageable moods. They moved slowly, in unison, below us, over the lawn, the boy, as they went, reading aloud from a storybook and passing his arm round his sister to keep her quite in touch. Mrs Grose watched them with positive placidity; then I caught the suppressed intellectual creak with which she conscientiously turned to take from me a view of the back of the tapestry. I had made her a receptacle of lurid things, but there was an odd recognition of my superiority – my accomplishments and my function – in her patience under my pain. She offered her mind to my disclosures as, had I wished to mix a witch's broth and proposed it with assurance, she would have held out a large, clean saucepan. This had become thoroughly her attitude by the time that, in my recital of the events of the night, I reached the point of what Miles had said to me when, after seeing him, at such a monstrous hour, almost on the very spot where he happened now to be, I had gone down to bring him in; choosing then, at the window with a concentrated need of not alarming the house, rather that method than any noisier process. I had left her meanwhile in little doubt of my small hope of representing with success even to her actual sympathy my sense of the real splendour of the little inspiration with which, after I had got him into the house, the boy met my final articulate challenge. As soon as I appeared in the moonlight on the terrace, he had come to me as straight as possible; on which I had taken his hand without a word and led him, through the dark spaces, up the staircase where Quint had so hungrily hovered for him, along the lobby where I had listened and trembled, and so to his forsaken room.

Not a sound, on the way, had passed between us and I had wondered – oh, *how* I had wondered! – if he were groping about in his dreadful little mind for something plausible and not too grotesque. It would tax his invention certainly, and I felt, this time, over his real embarrassment, a curious thrill of triumph. It was a sharp trap for any game hitherto successful. He could play no longer at perfect propriety, nor could he pretend to it; so how the deuce would he get out of the scrape? There beat in me indeed, with the passionate throb of this question, an equal dumb appeal as to how the deuce *I* should. I was confronted at last, as never yet, with all the risk attached even now to sounding my own horrid note. I remember, in fact, that as we pushed into his little chamber, where the bed had not been slept in at all and the window, uncovered to the moonlight, made the place so clear that there was no need of striking a match – I remember how I suddenly dropped, sank upon the edge of the bed from the force of the idea that he must know how he really, as they say, 'had' me. He could do what he liked, with all his cleverness to help him, so long as I should continue to defer to the old tradition of the criminality of those caretakers of the young who minister to superstitions and fears. He 'had' me indeed, and in a cleft stick; for who would ever absolve me, who would consent that I should be unhung, if, by the faintest tremor of an overture, I were the first to introduce into our perfect intercourse an element so dire? No, no: it was useless to attempt to convey to Mrs Grose, just as it is scarcely less so to attempt to suggest here, how, during our short, stiff brush there in the dark, he fairly shook me with admiration. I was of course thoroughly kind and merciful; never, never yet had I placed on his small shoulders hands of such tenderness as those with which, while I rested against the bed, I held him there well under fire. I had no alternative but, in form at least, to put it to him.

'You must tell me now – and all the truth. What did you go out for? What were you doing there?'

I can still see his wonderful smile, the whites of his beautiful eyes and the uncovering of his clear teeth, shine to me in the dusk. 'If I tell you why, will you understand?' My heart, at this, leaped into my mouth. *Would* he tell me why? I found no sound on my lips to press it, and I was aware of answering only with a vague, repeated, grimacing nod. He was gentleness itself, and while I wagged my head at him he stood there more than ever a little fairy prince. It was his brightness indeed that gave me a respite. Would it be so great if he were really going to tell me? 'Well,' he said at last, 'just exactly in order that you should do this.'

'Do what?'

'Think me – for a change – *bad*!' I shall never forget the sweetness and gaiety with which he brought out the word, nor how, on top of it, he bent forward and kissed me. It was practically the end of everything. I met his kiss and I had to make, while I folded him for a minute in my arms, the most stupendous effort not to cry. He had given exactly the account of himself that permitted least my going behind it, and it was only with the effect of confirming my acceptance of it that, as I presently glanced about the room, I could say: 'Then you didn't undress at all?'

He fairly glittered in the gloom. 'Not at all. I sat up and read.'

'And when did you go down?'

'At midnight. When I'm bad I *am* bad!'

'I see, I see – it's charming. But how could you be sure I should know it?'

'Oh, I arranged that with Flora.' His answers rang out with a readiness! 'She was to get up and look out.'

'Which is what she did do.' It was I who fell into the trap!

'So she disturbed you, and, to see what she was looking at, you also looked – you saw.'

'While you,' I concurred, 'caught your death in the night air!'

He literally bloomed so from this exploit that he could afford radiantly to assent. 'How otherwise should I have been bad enough?' he asked. Then, after another embrace, the incident and our interview closed on my recognition of all the reserves of goodness that, for his joke, he had been able to draw upon.

CHAPTER 12

The particular impression I had received proved in the morning light, I repeat, not quite successfully presentable to Mrs Grose, though I re-enforced it with the mention of still another remark that he had made before we separated. 'It all lies in half a dozen words,' I said to her, 'words that really settle the matter. "Think, you know, what I *might* do!" He threw that off to show me how good he is. He knows down to the ground what he "might do". That's what he gave them a taste of at school.'

'Lord, you do change!' cried my friend.

'I don't change – I simply make it out. The four, depend upon it, perpetually meet. If on either of these last nights you had been with either child you'd clearly have understood. The more I've watched and waited the more I've felt that if there were nothing else to make it sure it would be made so by the systematic silence of each. Never, by a slip of the tongue, have they so much as alluded to either of their old friends, any more than Miles has alluded to his expulsion. Oh, yes, we may sit here and look at them, and they may show off to us there to their fill; but even while they pretend to be lost in their fairytale they're steeped in their vision of the dead restored to them. He's not reading to her,' I declared; 'they're talking of *them* – they're talking horrors! I go on, I know, as if I were crazy; and it's a wonder I'm not. What I've seen would have made *you* so; but it has only made me more lucid, made me get hold of still other things.'

My lucidity must have seemed awful, but the

charming creatures who were victims of it, passing and repassing in their interlocked sweetness, gave my colleague something to hold on by; and I felt how tight she held as, without stirring in the breath of my passion, she covered them still with her eyes. 'Of what other things have you got hold?'

'Why, of the very things that have delighted, fascinated and yet, at bottom, as I now so strangely see, mystified and troubled me. Their more than earthly beauty, their absolutely unnatural goodness. It's a game,' I went on; 'it's a policy and a fraud!'

'On the part of little darlings – ?'

'As yet mere lovely babies? Yes, mad as that seems!' The very act of bringing it out really helped me to trace it – follow it all up and piece it all together. 'They haven't been good – they've only been absent. It has been easy to live with them because they're simply leading a life of their own. They're not mine – they're not ours. They're his and they're hers!'

'Quint's and that woman's?'

'Quint's and that woman's. They want to get to them.'

Oh, how, at this, poor Mrs Grose appeared to study them! 'But for what?'

'For the love of all the evil that, in those dreadful days, the pair put into them. And to ply them with that evil still, to keep up the work of demons, is what brings the others back.'

'Laws!' said my friend under her breath. The exclamation was homely, but it revealed a real acceptance of my further proof of what, in the bad time – for there had been a worse even than this – must have occurred. There could have been no such justification for me as the plain assent of her experience to whatever depth of depravity I found credible in our brace of scoundrels. It was in obvious submission of memory that she brought out after a moment: 'They *were* rascals! But what can they now do?' she pursued.

'Do?' I echoed so loud that Miles and Flora, as they passed at their distance, paused an instant in their walk and looked at us. 'Don't they do enough?' I demanded in a lower tone, while the children, having smiled and nodded and kissed hands to us, resumed their exhibition. We were held by it a minute; then I answered: 'They can destroy them!' At this my companion did turn, but the appeal she launched was a silent one, the effect of which was to make me more explicit. 'They don't know as yet quite how – but they're trying hard. They're seen only across, as it were, and beyond – in strange places and on high places, the top of towers, the roof of houses, the outside of windows, the farther edge of pools; but there's a deep design on either side, to shorten the distance and overcome the obstacle: so the success of the tempters is only a question of time. They've only to keep to their suggestions of danger.'

'For the children to come?'

'And perish in the attempt!' Mrs Grose slowly got up, and I scrupulously added: 'Unless, of course, we can prevent!'

Standing there before me while I kept my seat, she visibly turned things over. 'Their uncle must do the preventing. He must take them away.'

'And who's to make him?'

She had been scanning the distance, but she now dropped on me a foolish face. 'You, miss.'

'By writing to him that his house is poisoned and his nephew and niece mad?'

'But if they *are*, miss?'

'And if I am myself, you mean? That's charming news to be sent him by a person enjoying his confidence and whose prime undertaking was to give him no worry.'

Mrs Grose considered, following the children again. 'Yes, he do hate worry. That was the great reason – '

'Why those fiends took him in so long? No doubt, though his indifference must have been awful. As I'm not a fiend, at any rate, I shouldn't take him in.'

My companion, after an instant and for all answer, sat down again and grasped my arm. 'Make him at any rate come to you.'

I stared. 'To *me*?' I had a sudden fear of what she might do. ' "Him"? '

'He ought to *be* here – he ought to help.'

I quickly rose and I think I must have shown her a queerer face than ever yet. 'You see me asking him for a visit?' No, with her eyes on my face she evidently couldn't. Instead of it even – as a woman reads another – she could see what I myself saw: his derision, his amusement, his contempt for the breakdown of my resignation at being left alone and for the fine machinery I had set in motion to attract his attention to my slighted charms. She didn't know – no one knew – how proud I had been to serve him and to stick to our terms; yet she none the less took the measure, I think, of the warning I now gave her. 'If you should so lose your head as to appeal to him for me – '

She was really frightened. 'Yes, miss?'

'I would leave, on the spot, both him and you.'

CHAPTER 13

It was all very well to join them, but speaking to them proved quite as much as ever an effort beyond my strength – offered, in close quarters, difficulties as insurmountable as before. This situation continued a month, and with new aggravations and particular notes, the note above all, sharper and sharper, of the small ironic consciousness on the part of my pupils. It was not, I am as sure today as I was sure then, my mere infernal imagination: it was absolutely traceable that they were aware of my predicament and that this strange relation made, in a manner, for a long time, the air in which we moved. I don't mean that they had their tongues in their cheeks or did anything vulgar, for that was not one of their dangers: I do mean, on the other hand, that the element of the unnamed and untouched became, between us, greater than any other, and that so much avoidance couldn't have been made successful without a great deal of tacit arrangement. It was as if, at moments, we were perpetually coming into sight of subjects before which we must stop short, turning suddenly out of alleys that we perceived to be blind, closing with a little bang that made us look at each other – for, like all bangs, it was something louder than we had intended – the doors we had indiscreetly opened. All roads lead to Rome, and there were times when it might have struck us that almost every branch of study or subject of conversation skirted forbidden ground. Forbidden ground was the question of the return of the dead in general and of whatever, especially, might survive, for memory, of the friends little children had lost. There were days when I could have sworn that one of them had, with a small invisible nudge, said to the other: 'She thinks she'll do it this time – but she *won't*!' To 'do it' would have been to indulge, for instance – and for once in a way – in some direct reference to the lady who had prepared them for my discipline. They had a delightful endless appetite for passages in my own history to which I had again and again treated them; they were in possession of everything that had ever happened to me, had had, with every circumstance, the story of my smallest adventures and of those of my brothers and sisters and of the cat and the dog at home, as well as many particulars of the whimsical bent of my father, of the furniture and arrangement of our house and of the conversation of the old women of our village. There were things enough, taking one with another, to chatter about, if one went very fast and knew by instinct when to go round. They pulled with an art of their own the strings of my invention and my memory; and nothing else perhaps, when I thought of such occasions afterwards, gave me so the suspicion of being watched from under cover. It was in any case over *my* life, *my* past and *my* friends alone that we could take anything like our ease; a state of affairs that led them sometimes without the least pertinence to break out into sociable reminders. I was invited – with no visible connection – to repeat afresh Goody Gosling's celebrated *mot* or to confirm the details already supplied as to the cleverness of the vicarage pony.

It was partly at such junctures as these and partly at quite different ones that, with the turn my matters had now taken, my predicament, as I have called it, grew most sensible. The fact that the days passed for me without another encounter ought, it would have appeared, to have done something towards soothing my nerves. Since the light brush, that second night on the upper landing, of the presence of a woman at the foot of the stair, I had seen nothing, whether in or out of the house, that one had better not have seen. There was many a corner round which I expected to come upon Quint, and many a situation that, in a merely sinister way, would have favoured the appearance of Miss Jessel. The summer had turned, the summer had gone; the autumn had dropped upon Bly and had blown out half our lights. The place, with its grey sky and withered garlands, its bared spaces and scattered dead leaves, was like a theatre after the performance – all strewn with crumpled playbills. There were exactly states of the air, conditions of sound and of stillness, unspeakable impressions of the *kind* of ministering moment, that brought back to me, long enough to catch it, the feeling of the medium in which, that June evening out of doors, I had had my first sight of Quint, and in which too, at those other instants, I had, after seeing him through the window, looked for him in vain in the circle of shrubbery. I recognised the signs, the portents – I recognised the moment, the spot. But they remained unaccompanied and empty, and I continued unmolested; if unmolested one could call a young woman whose sensibility had, in the most extraordinary fashion, not declined but deepened. I had said in my talk with Mrs Grose on that horrid scene of Flora's by the lake – and had perplexed her by so saying – that it would from that moment distress me much more to lose my power than to keep it. I had then expressed what was vividly in my mind: the truth that, whether the children really saw or not – since, that is, it was not yet definitely proved – I greatly preferred, as a safeguard, the fullness of my own exposure. I was ready to know the very worst that was to be known. What I had then had an ugly glimpse of was that my eyes might be sealed just while theirs were most opened. Well, my eyes *were* sealed, it appeared, at present – a consummation for which it seemed blasphemous not to thank God. There was, alas, a difficulty about that: I would have thanked Him with all my soul had I not had in a proportionate measure this conviction of the secret of my pupils.

How can I retrace today the strange steps of my obsession? There were times of our being together when I would have been ready to swear that, literally, in my presence, but with my direct sense of it closed, they had visitors who were known and were welcome. Then it was that, had I not been deterred by the very chance that such an injury might prove greater than the injury to be averted, my exaltation would have broken out. 'They're here, they're here, you little wretches,' I would have cried, 'and you can't deny it now!' The little wretches denied it with all the added volume of their sociability and their tenderness, just in the crystal depths of which – like the flash of a fish in a stream – the mockery of their advantage peeped up. The shock had in truth sunk into me still deeper than I knew on the night when, looking out either for Quint or for Miss Jessel under the stars, I had seen there the boy over whose rest I watched and who had immediately brought in with him – had straightaway there turned on me – the lovely upward look with which, from the battlements above us, the hideous apparition of Quint had played. If it was a question of a scare, my discovery on this occasion had scared me more than any other, and it was essentially in the scared state that I drew my actual conclusions. They harassed me so that sometimes, at odd moments, I shut myself up audibly to rehearse – it was at once a fantastic relief and a renewed despair – the manner in which I might come to the point. I approached it from one side and the other while, in my room, I flung myself about, but I always broke down in the monstrous utterances of names. As they died away on my lips I said to myself that I should indeed help them to represent something infamous if by pronouncing them I should violate as rare a little case of instinctive delicacy as any schoolroom probably had ever known. When I said to myself: '*They* have the manners to be silent, and you, trusted as you are, the baseness to speak!' I felt myself crimson and covered my face with my hands. After these secret scenes I chattered more than ever, going on volubly enough till one of our prodigious, palpable hushes occurred – I can call them nothing else – the strange, dizzy lift or swim (I try for terms!) into a stillness, a pause of all life, that had nothing to do with the more or less noise we at the moment might be engaged in making and that I could hear through any intensified mirth or quickened recitation or louder strum of the piano. Then it was that the others, the outsiders, were there. Though they were not angels they 'passed', as the French say, causing me, while they stayed, to tremble with the fear of their addressing to their younger victims some yet more infernal message or more vivid image than they had thought good enough for myself.

What it was least possible to get rid of was the cruel idea that, whatever I had seen, Miles and Flora saw *more* – things terrible and unguessable and that sprang from dreadful passages of intercourse in the past. Such things naturally left on the surface, for the time, a chill that we vociferously denied we felt; and we had all three, with repetition, got into such splendid training that we went, each time, to mark the close of the incident, almost automatically through the very same movements. It was striking of the children at all events to kiss me inveterately with a wild irrelevance and never to fail – one or the other – of the precious question that had helped us through many a peril. 'When do you think he *will* come? Don't you think we *ought* to write?' – there was nothing like that inquiry, we found by experience, for carrying off an awkwardness. 'He', of course, was their uncle in Harley Street; and we lived in much profusion of theory that he might at any moment arrive to mingle in our circle. It was impossible to have given less encouragement than he had administered to such a doctrine, but if we had not had the doctrine to fall back upon, we should have deprived each other of some of our finest exhibitions. He never wrote to them – that may have been selfish, but it was a part of the flattery of his trust of myself; for the way in which a man pays his highest tribute to a woman is apt to be but by the more festal celebration of one of the sacred laws of his comfort. So I held that I carried out the spirit of the pledge given not to appeal to him when I let our young friends understand that their own letters were but charming literary exercises. They were too beautiful to be posted; I kept them myself; I have them all to this hour. This was a rule, indeed, which only added to the satiric effect of my being plied with the supposition that he might at any moment be among us. It was exactly as if our young friends knew how almost more awkward than anything else that might be for me. There appears to me, moreover, as I look back, no note in all this more extraordinary than the mere fact that, in spite of my tension and of their triumph, I never lost patience with them. Adorable they must in truth have been, I now feel, since I didn't in these days hate them! Would exasperation, however, if relief had longer been postponed, finally have betrayed me? It little matters, for relief arrived. I call it relief though it was only the relief that a snap brings to a strain or the burst of a thunderstorm to a day of suffocation. It was at least change, and it came with a rush.

CHAPTER 14

Walking to church a certain Sunday morning, I had little Miles at my side and his sister, in advance of us and at Mrs Grose's, well in sight. It was a crisp, clear day, the first of its order for some time; the night had brought a touch of frost and the autumn air, bright and sharp, made the church bells almost gay. It was an odd accident of thought that I should have happened at such a moment to be particularly and very gratefully struck with the obedience of my little charges. Why did they never resent my inexorable, my perpetual society? Something or other had brought nearer home to me that I had all but pinned the boy to my shawl, and that in the way our companions were marshalled before me I might have appeared to provide against some danger of rebellion. I was like a jailer with an eye to possible surprises and escapes. But all this belonged – I mean their magnificent little surrender – just to the special array of the facts that were most abysmal. Turned out for Sunday by his uncle's tailor, who had had a free hand and a notion of pretty waistcoats and of his grand little air, Miles's whole title to independence, the rights of his sex and situation, were so stamped upon him that if he had suddenly struck for freedom I should have had nothing to say. I was by the strangest of chances wondering how I should meet him when the revolution unmistakably occurred. I call it a revolution because I now see how, with the word he spoke, the curtain rose on the last act of my dreadful drama and the catastrophe was precipitated. 'Look here, my dear, you know,' he charmingly said, 'when in the world, please, am I going back to school?'

Transcribed here the speech sounds harmless enough, particularly as uttered in the sweet, high, casual pipe with which, at all interlocutors, but above all at his eternal governess, he threw off intonations as if he were tossing roses. There was something in them that always made one 'catch', and I caught at any rate now so effectually that I stopped as short as if one of the trees of the park had fallen across the road. There was something new, on the spot, between us, and he was perfectly aware I recognised it, though to enable me to do so he had no need to look a whit less candid and charming than usual. I could feel in him how he already, from my at first finding nothing to reply, perceived the advantage he had gained. I was so slow to find anything that he had plenty of time, after a minute, to continue with his suggestive but inconclusive smile: 'You know, my dear, that for a fellow to be with a lady *always* – !' His 'my dear' was constantly on his lips for me, and nothing could have expressed more the exact shade of the sentiment with which I desired to inspire my pupils than its fond familiarity. It was so respectfully easy.

But oh, how I felt that at present I must pick my own phrases! I remember that, to gain time, I tried to laugh, and I seemed to see in the beautiful face with which he watched me how ugly and queer I looked. 'And always with the same lady?' I returned.

He neither blenched nor winked. The whole thing was virtually out between us. 'Ah, of course she's a jolly "perfect" lady; but after all I'm a fellow, don't you see? who's – well, getting on.'

I lingered there with him an instant ever so kindly. 'Yes, you're getting on.' Oh, but I felt helpless!

I have kept to this day the heartbreaking little idea of how he seemed to know that and to play with it. 'And you can't say I've not been awfully good, can you?'

I laid my hand on his shoulder, for though I felt how much better it would have been to walk on, I was not yet quite able. 'No, I can't say that, Miles.'

'Except just that one night, you know – !'

'That one night?' I couldn't look as straight as he.

'Why, when I went down – went out of the house.'

'Oh, yes. But I forget what you did it for.'

'You forget?' – he spoke with the sweet extravagance of childish reproach. 'Why, it was just to show you I could!'

'Oh, yes – you could.'

'And I can again.'

I felt I might perhaps after all succeed in keeping my wits about me. 'Certainly. But you won't.'

'No, not *that* again. It was nothing.'

'It was nothing,' I said. 'But we must go on.'

He resumed our walk with me, passing his hand into my arm. 'Then when *am* I going back?'

I wore, in turning it over, my most responsible air. 'Were you very happy at school?'

He just considered. 'Oh, I'm happy enough anywhere!'

'Well, then,' I quavered, 'if you're just as happy here – !'

'Ah, but that isn't everything! Of course *you* know a lot – '

'But you hint that you know almost as much?' I asked as he paused.

'Not half I want to!' Miles honestly professed. 'But it isn't so much that.'

'What is it, then?'

'Well – I want to see more life.'

'I see; I see.' We had arrived within sight of the church and of various persons, including several of the household of Bly, on their way to it and clustered about the door to see us go in. I quickened our step; I wanted to get there before the question between us opened up much further; I reflected hungrily that he would have for more than an hour to be silent, and I thought with envy of the comparative dusk of the pew and of the almost spiritual help of the hassock on which I might bend my knees. I seemed literally to be running a race with some confusion to which he was about to reduce me, but I felt he had got in first when, before we had entered the churchyard, he threw out: 'I want my own sort!'

It literally made me bound forward. 'There aren't many of your own sort, Miles!' I laughed. 'Unless perhaps dear little Flora!'

'You really compare me to a baby girl?'

This found me singularly weak. 'Don't you then *love* our sweet Flora?'

'If I didn't – and you too; if I didn't – !' he repeated as if retreating for a jump, yet leaving his thought so unfinished that, after we had come into the gate, another stop, which he imposed on me by the pressure of his arm, had become inevitable. Mrs Grose and Flora had passed into the church, the other worshippers had followed and we were, for the minute, alone among the old, thick graves. We had paused, on the path from the gate, by a low, oblong, table-like tomb.

'Yes, if you didn't – ?'

He looked, while I waited, about at the graves.

'Well, you know what!' But he didn't move, and he presently produced something that made me drop straight down on the stone slab as if suddenly to rest. 'Does my uncle think what *you* think?'

I markedly rested. 'How do you know what I think?'

'Ah, well, of course I don't; for it strikes me you never tell me. But I mean does *he* know?'

'Know what, Miles?'

'Why, the way I'm going on.'

I recognised quickly enough that I could make, to this inquiry, no answer that wouldn't involve something of a sacrifice of my employer. Yet it struck me that we were all, at Bly, sufficiently sacrificed to make that venial. 'I don't think your uncle much cares.'

Miles, on this, stood looking at me. 'Then don't you think he can be made to?'

'In what way?'

'Why, by his coming down.'

'But who'll get him to come down?'

'*I* will!' the boy said with extraordinary brightness and emphasis. He gave me another look charged with that expression and then marched off alone into church.

CHAPTER 15

The business was practically settled from the moment I never followed him. It was a pitiful surrender to agitation, but my being aware of this had somehow no power to restore me. I only sat there on my tomb and read into what our young friend had said to me the fullness of its meaning; by the time I had grasped the whole of which, I had also embraced, for absence, the pretext that I was ashamed to offer my pupils and the rest of the congregation such an example of delay. What I said to myself, above all, was that Miles had got something out of me and that the gauge of it for him would be just this awkward collapse. He had got out of me that there was something I was much afraid of, and that he should probably be able to make use of my fear to gain, for his own purpose, more freedom. My fear was of having to deal with the intolerable question of the grounds of his dismissal from school, since that was really but the question of the horrors gathered behind. That his uncle should arrive to treat with me of these things was a solution that, strictly speaking, I ought now to have desired to bring on; but I could so little face the ugliness and the pain of it that I simply procrastinated and lived from hand to mouth. The boy, to my deep discomposure, was immensely in the right, was in a position to say to me: 'Either you clear up with my guardian the mystery of this interruption of my studies, or you cease to expect me to lead with you a life that's so unnatural for a boy.' What was so unnatural for the particular boy I was concerned with was this sudden revelation of a consciousness and a plan.

That was what really overcame me, what prevented my going in. I walked round the church hesitating, hovering; I reflected that I had already, with him, hurt myself beyond repair. Therefore I could patch up nothing and it was too extreme an effort to squeeze beside him into the pew: he would be so much more sure than ever to pass his arm into mine and make me sit there for an hour in close silent contact with his commentary on our talk. For the first minute since his arrival, I wanted to get away from him. As I paused beneath the high east window and listened to the sounds of worship, I was taken with an impulse that might master me, I felt, and completely, should I give it the least encouragement. I might easily put an end to my ordeal by getting away altogether. Here was my chance; there was no one to stop me; I could give the whole thing up – turn my back and bolt. It was only a question of hurrying again, for a few preparations, to the house which the attendance at church of so many of the servants would practically have left unoccupied. No one, in short, could blame me if I should just drive desperately off. What was it to get away if I should get away only till dinner? That would be in a couple of hours, at the end of which – I had the acute prevision – my little pupils would play at innocent wonder about my non-appearance in their train.

'What *did* you do, you naughty bad thing? Why in

the world, to worry us so – and take our thoughts off too, don't you know? – did you desert us at the very door?' I couldn't meet such questions nor, as they asked them, their false little lovely eyes; yet it was all so exactly what I should have to meet that, as the prospect grew sharp to me, I at last let myself go.

I got, so far as the immediate moment was concerned, away; I came straight out of the churchyard and, thinking hard, retraced my steps through the park. It seemed to me that by the time I reached the house I had made up my mind to cynical flight. The Sunday stillness both of the approaches and of the interior, in which I met no one, fairly stirred me with a sense of opportunity. Were I to get off quickly this way I should get off without a scene, without a word. My quickness would have to be remarkable, however, and the question of a conveyance was the great one to settle. Tormented, in the hall, with difficulties and obstacles, I remember sinking down at the foot of the staircase – suddenly collapsing there on the lowest step and then, with a revulsion, recalling that it was exactly where, more than a month before, in the darkness of night and just so bowed with evil things, I had seen the spectre of the most horrible of women. At this I was able to straighten myself; I went the rest of the way up; I made, in my turmoil, for the school-room, where there were objects belonging to me that I should have to take. But I opened the door to find again, in a flash, my eyes unsealed. In the presence of what I saw, I reeled straight back upon resistance.

Seated at my own table in the clear noonday light I saw a person whom, without my previous experience, I should have taken at the first blush for some housemaid who might have stayed at home to look after the place and who, availing herself of rare relief from observation and of the schoolroom table and my pens, ink, and paper, had applied herself to the considerable effort of a letter to her sweetheart. There was an effort in the way that, while her arms rested on the table, her hands, with evident weariness, supported her head; but at the moment I took this in I had already become aware that, in spite of my entrance, her attitude strangely persisted. Then it was – with the very act of its announcing itself – that her identity flared up in a change of posture. She rose, not as if she had heard me, but with an indescribable grand melancholy of indifference and detachment, and, within a dozen feet of me, stood there as my vile predecessor. Dishonoured and tragic, she was all before me; but even as I fixed and, for memory, secured it, the awful image passed away. Dark as midnight in her dark dress, her haggard beauty and her unutterable woe, she had looked at me long enough to appear to say that her right to sit at my table was as good as mine to sit at hers. While these instants lasted indeed I had the extraordinary chill of a feeling that it was I who was the intruder. It was as a wild protest against it that, actually addressing her – 'You terrible, miserable woman!' – I heard myself break into a sound that, by the open door, rang through the long passage and the empty house. She looked at me as if she heard me, but I had recovered myself and cleared the air. There was nothing in the room the next minute but the sunshine and the sense that I must stay.

CHAPTER 16

I had so perfectly expected the return of the others to be marked by a demonstration that I was freshly upset at having to find them merely dumb and discreet about my desertion. Instead of gaily denouncing and caressing me they made no allusion to my having failed them, and I was left, for the time, on perceiving that she too said nothing, to study Mrs Grose's odd face. I did this to such purpose that I made sure they had in some way bribed her to silence; a silence that, however, I would engage to break down on the first private opportunity. This opportunity came before tea: I secured five minutes with her in the house-keeper's room, where, in the twilight, amid a smell of lately-baked bread, but with the place all swept and garnished, I found her sitting in pained placidity before the fire. So I see her still, so I see her best: facing the flame from her straight chair in the dusky, shining room, a large, clean picture of the 'put away' – of drawers closed and locked and rest without a remedy.

'Oh, yes, they asked me to say nothing; and to please them – so long as they were there – of course I promised. But what had happened to you?'

'I only went with you for the walk,' I said. 'I had then to come back to meet a friend.'

She showed her surprise. 'A friend – *you*?'

'Oh, yes, I've a couple!' I laughed. 'But did the children give you a reason?'

'For not alluding to your leaving us? Yes; they said you'd like it better. *Do* you like it better?'

My face had made her rueful. 'No, I like it worse!' But after an instant I added: 'Did they say why I should like it better?'

'No; Master Miles only said, "We must do nothing but what she likes"!'

'I wish indeed he would! And what did Flora say?'

'Miss Flora was too sweet. She said, "Oh, of course, of course!" – and I said the same.'

I thought a moment. 'You were too sweet, too – I can hear you all. But none the less, between Miles and me, it's now all out.'

'All out?' My companion stared. 'But what, miss?'

'Everything. It doesn't matter. I've made up my mind. I came home, my dear,' I went on, 'for a talk with Miss Jessel.'

I had by this time formed the habit of having Mrs Grose literally well in hand in advance of my sounding that note; so that even now, as she bravely blinked under the signal of my word, I could keep her comparatively firm. 'A talk! Do you mean she spoke?'

'It came to that. I found her, on my return, in the schoolroom.'

'And what did she say?' I can hear the good woman still, and the candour of her stupefaction.

'That she suffers the torments – !'

It was this, of a truth, that made her, as she filled out my picture, gape. 'Do you mean,' she faltered ' – of the lost?'

'Of the lost. Of the damned. And that's why, to share them – ' I faltered myself with the horror of it.

But my companion, with less imagination, kept me up. 'To share them – ?'

'She wants Flora.' Mrs Grose might, as I gave it to her, fairly have fallen away from me had I not been prepared. I still held her there, to show I was. 'As I've told you, however, it doesn't matter.'

'Because you've made up your mind? But to what?'

'To everything.'

'And what do you call "everything"?'

'Why, to sending for their uncle.'

'Oh, miss, in pity do,' my friend broke out.

'Ah, but I will, I *will*! I see it's the only way. What's "out", as I told you, with Miles is that if he thinks I'm afraid to – and has ideas of what he gains by that – he shall see he's mistaken. Yes, yes, his uncle shall have it here from me on the spot (and before the boy himself if necessary) that if I'm to be reproached with having done nothing again about more school – '

'Yes, miss – ' my companion pressed me.

'Well, there's that awful reason.'

There were now clearly so many of these for my poor colleague that she was excusable for being vague. 'But – a – which?'

'Why, the letter from his old place.'

'You'll show it to the master?'

'I ought to have done so on the instant.'

'Oh, no!' said Mrs Grose with decision.

'I'll put it before him,' I went on inexorably, 'that I can't undertake to work the question on behalf of a child who has been expelled – '

'For we've never in the least known what!' Mrs Grose declared.

'For wickedness. For what else – when he's so clever and beautiful and perfect? Is he stupid? Is he untidy? Is he infirm? Is he ill-natured? He's exquisite – so it can be only *that*; and that would open up the whole thing. After all,' I said, 'it's their uncle's fault. If he left here such people – !'

'He didn't really in the least know them. The fault's mine.' She had turned quite pale.

'Well, you shan't suffer,' I answered.

'The children shan't!' she emphatically returned.

I was silent awhile; we looked at each other. 'Then what am I to tell him?'

'You needn't tell him anything. *I'll* tell him.'

I measured this. 'Do you mean you'll write – ?' Remembering she couldn't, I caught myself up. 'How do you communicate?'

'I tell the bailiff. *He* writes.'

'And should you like him to write our story?'

My question had a sarcastic force that I had not fully intended, and it made her after a moment inconsequently break down. The tears were again in her eyes. 'Ah, miss, you write!'

'Well – tonight,' I at last returned; and on this we separated.

CHAPTER 17

I went so far, in the evening, as to make a beginning. The weather had changed back, a great wind was abroad, and beneath the lamp, in my room, with Flora at peace beside me, I sat for a long time before a blank sheet of paper and listened to the lash of the rain and the batter of the gusts. Finally I went out, taking a candle; I crossed the passage and listened a minute at Miles's door. What, under my endless obsession, I had been impelled to listen for was some betrayal of his not being at rest, and I presently caught one, but not in the form I had expected. His voice tinkled out. 'I say, you there – come in.' It was gaiety in the gloom!

I went in with my light and found him in bed, very wide awake but very much at his ease. 'Well, what are *you* up to?' he asked with a grace of sociability in which it occurred to me that Mrs Grose, had she been present, might have looked in vain for proof that anything was 'out'.

I stood over him with my candle. 'How did you know I was there?'

'Why, of course, I heard you. Did you fancy you made no noise? You're like a troop of cavalry!' he beautifully laughed.

'Then you weren't asleep?'

'Not much! I lie awake and think.'

I had put my candle, designedly, a short way off, and then, as he held out his friendly old hand to me, had sat down on the edge of his bed. 'What is it,' I asked, 'that you think of?'

'What in the world, my dear, but *you*?'

'Ah, the pride I take in your appreciation doesn't insist on that! I had so far rather you slept.'

'Well, I think also, you know, of this queer business of ours.'

I marked the coolness of his firm little hand. 'Of what queer business, Miles?'

'Why, the way you bring me up. And all the rest!'

I fairly held my breath a minute, and even from my glimmering taper there was light enough to show how he smiled up at me from his pillow. 'What do you mean by all the rest?'

'Oh, you know, you know!'

I could say nothing for a minute, though I felt as I held his hand and our eyes continued to meet that my silence had all the air of admitting his charge and that nothing in the whole world of reality was perhaps at that moment so fabulous as our actual relation. 'Certainly you shall go back to school,' I said, 'if it be that that troubles you. But not to the old place – we must find another, a better. How could I know it did trouble you, this question, when you never told me so, never spoke of it at all?' His clear listening face, framed in its smooth whiteness, made him for the minute as appealing as some wistful patient in a children's hospital; and I would have given, as the resemblance came to me, all I possessed on earth really to be the nurse or the sister of charity who might have helped to cure him. Well, even as it was I perhaps might help! 'Do you know you've never said a word to me about your school – I mean the old one; never mentioned it in any way?'

He seemed to wonder; he smiled with the same loveliness. But he clearly gained time; he waited, he called for guidance. 'Haven't I?' It wasn't for *me* to help him – it was for the thing I had met!

Something in his tone and the expression of his face, as I got this from him, set my heart aching with such a pang as it had never yet known; so unutterably touching was it to see his little brain puzzled and his little resources taxed to play, under the spell laid on him, a part of innocence and consistency. 'No, never – from the hour you came back. You've never mentioned to me one of your masters, one of your comrades, nor the least little thing that ever happened to you at school. Never, little Miles – no, never – have you given me an inkling of anything that *may* have happened there. Therefore you can fancy how much I'm in the dark. Until you came out, that way, this morning, you had since the first hour I saw you scarce even made a reference to anything in your previous

life. You seemed so perfectly to accept the present.'
It was extraordinary how my absolute conviction of
his secret precocity – or whatever I might call the
poison of an influence that I dared but half-phrase –
made him, in spite of the faint breath of his inward
trouble, appear as accessible as an older person,
forced me to treat him as an intelligent equal. 'I
thought you wanted to go on as you are.'

It struck me that at this he just faintly coloured. He
gave, at any rate, like a convalescent slightly fatigued,
a languid shake of his head. 'I don't – I don't. I want
to get away.'

'You're tired of Bly?'

'Oh, no, I like Bly.'

'Well, then – ?'

'Oh, *you* know what a boy wants!'

I felt I didn't know so well as Miles, and I took
temporary refuge. 'You want to go to your uncle?'

Again, at this, with his sweet ironic face, he made a
movement on the pillow. 'Ah, you can't get off with
that!'

I was silent a little, and it was I now, I think, who
changed colour. 'My dear, I don't want to get off!'

'You can't even if you do. You can't, you can't!' –
he lay beautifully staring. 'My uncle must come down
and you must completely settle things.'

'If we do,' I returned with some spirit, 'you may be
sure it will be to take you quite away.'

'Well, don't you understand that that's exactly what
I'm working for? You'll have to *tell* him – about the
way you've let it all drop: you'll have to tell him a
tremendous lot!'

The exultation with which he uttered this helped
me somehow for the instant to meet him rather more.

'And how much will *you*, Miles, have to tell him? There are things he'll ask you!'

He turned it over. 'Very likely. But what things?'

'The things you've never told me. To make up his mind what to do with you. He can't send you back – '

'I don't want to go back!' he broke in. 'I want a new field.'

He said it with admirable serenity, with positive, unimpeachable gaiety; and doubtless it was that very note that most evoked for me the poignancy, the unnatural childish tragedy, of his probable reappearance at the end of three months with all this bravado and still more dishonour. It overwhelmed me now that I should never be able to bear that, and it made me let myself go. I threw myself upon him and in the tenderness of my pity embraced him. 'Dear little Miles, dear little Miles – !'

My face was close to his, and he let me kiss him, simply taking it with indulgent good humour. 'Well, old lady?'

'Is there nothing – nothing at all that you want to tell me?'

He turned off a little, facing round towards the wall and holding up his hand to look at as one had seen sick children look. 'I've told you – I told you this morning.'

Oh, I was sorry for him! 'That you just want me not to worry you?'

He looked round at me now as if in recognition of my understanding him; then ever so gently, 'To let me alone,' he replied.

There was even a strange little dignity in it, something that made me release him, yet, when I had slowly risen, linger beside him. God knows I never wished to harass him, but I felt that merely, at this, to turn my back on him was to abandon or, to put it more truly, to lose him. 'I've just begun a letter to your uncle,' I said.

'Well, then, finish it!'

I waited a minute. 'What happened before?'

He gazed up at me again. 'Before what?'

'Before you came back. And before you went away.'

For some time he was silent, but he continued to meet my eyes. 'What happened?'

It made me, the sound of the words, in which it seemed to me I caught for the very first time a small faint quaver of consenting consciousness – it made me drop to my knees beside the bed and seize once more the chance of possessing him. 'Dear little Miles, dear little Miles, if you knew how I want to help you! It's only that, it's nothing but that, and I'd rather die than give you a pain or do you a wrong – I'd rather die than hurt a hair of you. Dear little Miles' – oh I brought it out now even if I *should* go too far – 'I just want you to help me to save you!' But I knew in a moment after this that I had gone too far. The answer to my appeal was instantaneous, but it came in the form of an extraordinary blast and chill, a gust of frozen air and a shake of the room as great as if, in the wild wind, the casement had crashed in. The boy gave a loud, high shriek which, lost in the rest of the shock of sound, might have seemed, indistinctly, though I was so close to him, a note either of jubilation or of terror. I jumped to my feet again and was conscious of darkness. So for a moment we remained, while I stared about me and saw the drawn curtains unstirred and the window tight. 'Why, the candle's out!' I then cried.

'It was I who blew it, dear!' said Miles.

CHAPTER 18

The next day, after lessons, Mrs Grose found a moment to say to me quietly: 'Have you written, miss?'

'Yes – I've written.' But I didn't add – for the hour – that my letter, sealed and directed, was still in my pocket. There would be time enough to send it before the messenger should go to the village. Meanwhile there had been on the part of my pupils no more brilliant, more exemplary morning. It was exactly as if they had both had at heart to gloss over any recent little friction. They performed the dizziest feats of arithmetic, soaring quite out of *my* feeble range, and perpetrated, in higher spirits than ever, geographical and historical jokes. It was conspicuous of course in Miles in particular that he appeared to wish to show how easily he could let me down. This child, to my memory, really lives in a setting of beauty and misery that no words can translate; there was a distinction all his own in every impulse he revealed; never was a small natural creature, to the uninformed eye all frankness and freedom, a more ingenious, a more extraordinary little gentleman. I had perpetually to guard against the wonder of contemplation into which my initiated view betrayed me; to check the irrelevant gaze and discouraged sigh in which I constantly both attacked and renounced the enigma of what such a little gentleman could have done that deserved a penalty. Say that, by the dark prodigy I knew, the imagination of all evil had been opened up to him: all the justice within me ached for the proof that it could ever have flowered into an act.

He had never at any rate been such a little gentleman as when, after our early dinner on this dreadful day, he came round to me and asked if I shouldn't like him for half an hour to play to me. David playing to Saul could never have shown a finer sense of the occasion. It was literally a charming exhibition of tact, of magnanimity, and quite tantamount to his saying outright: 'The true knights we love to read about never push an advantage too far. I know what you mean now: you mean that – to be let alone yourself and not followed up – you'll cease to worry and spy upon me, won't keep me so close to you, will let me go and come. Well, I "come", you see – but I don't go! There'll be plenty of time for that. I do really delight in your society and I only want to show you that I contended for a principle.' It may be imagined whether I resisted this appeal or failed to accompany him again, hand in hand, to the school-room. He sat down at the old piano and played as he had never played; and if there are those who think he had better have been kicking a football, I can only say that I wholly agree with them. For at the end of a time that under his influence I had quite ceased to measure, I started up with a strange sense of having literally slept at my post. It was after luncheon, and by the schoolroom fire, and yet I hadn't really in the least slept; I had only done something much worse – I had forgotten. Where all this time was Flora? When I put the question to Miles, he played on a minute before answering, and then could only say: 'Why, my dear, how do *I* know?' – breaking moreover into a happy laugh which immediately after, as if it were a vocal accompaniment, he prolonged into incoherent, extravagant song.

I went straight to my room, but his sister was not there; then, before going downstairs, I looked into several others. As she was nowhere about she would surely be with Mrs Grose, whom in the comfort of that theory I accordingly proceeded in quest of. I found her where I had found her the evening before, but she met my quick challenge with blank scared ignorance. She had only supposed that, after the repast, I had carried off both the children; as to which she was quite in her right, for it was the very first time I had allowed the little girl out of my sight without some special provision. Of course now indeed she might be with the maids, so that the immediate thing was to look for her without an air of alarm. This we promptly arranged between us; but when, ten minutes later and in pursuance of our arrangement, we met in the hall, it was only to report on either side that after guarded inquiries we had altogether failed to trace her. For a minute there, apart from observation, we exchanged mute alarms, and I could feel with what high interest my friend returned me all those I had from the first given her.

'She'll be above,' she presently said – 'in one of the rooms you haven't searched.'

'No; she's at a distance.' I had made up my mind. 'She has gone out.'

Mrs Grose stared. 'Without a hat!'

I naturally also looked volumes. 'Isn't that woman always without one?'

'She's with *her*?'

'She's with *her*!' I declared. 'We must find them.'

My hand was on my friend's arm, but she failed for

the moment, confronted with such an account of the matter, to respond to my pressure. She communed on the contrary, where she stood, with her uneasiness. 'And where's Master Miles?'

'Oh, *he's* with Quint. They'll be in the school-room.'

'Lord, miss!' My view, I was myself aware – and therefore I suppose my tone – had never yet reached so calm an assurance.

'The trick's played,' I went on; 'they've successfully worked their plan. He found the most divine little way to keep me quiet while she went off.'

' "Divine"?' Mrs Grose bewilderedly echoed.

'Infernal, then!' I almost cheerfully rejoined. 'He has provided for himself as well. But come!'

She had helplessly gloomed at the upper regions. 'You leave him – ?'

'So long with Quint? Yes – I don't mind that now.'

She always ended at these moments by getting possession of my hand, and in this manner she could at present still stay me. But after gasping an instant at my sudden resignation, 'Because of your letter?' she eagerly brought out.

I quickly, by way of answer, felt for my letter, drew it forth, held it up, and then, freeing myself, went and laid it on the great hall-table. 'Luke will take it,' I said as I came back. I reached the house-door and opened it; I was already on the steps.

My companion still demurred: the storm of the night and the early morning had dropped, but the afternoon was damp and grey. I came down to the drive while she stood in the doorway. 'You go with nothing on?'

'What do I care when the child has nothing? I can't

wait to dress,' I cried, 'and if you must do so I leave you. Try meanwhile yourself upstairs.'

'With *them*?' Oh, on this the poor woman promptly joined me!

CHAPTER 19

We went straight to the lake, as it was called at Bly, and I dare say rightly called, though it may have been a sheet of water less remarkable than my untravelled eyes supposed it. My acquaintance with sheets of water was small, and the pool of Bly, at all events on the few occasions of my consenting, under the protection of my pupils, to affront its surface in the old flat-bottomed boat moored there for our use, had impressed me both with its extent and its agitation. The usual place of embarkation was half a mile from the house, but I had an intimate conviction that, wherever Flora might be, she was not near home. She had not given me the slip for any small adventure, and, since the day of the very great one that I had shared with her by the pond, I had been aware, in our walks, of the quarter to which she most inclined. This was why I had now given to Mrs Grose's steps so marked a direction – a direction making her, when she perceived it, oppose a resistance that showed me she was freshly mystified. 'You're going to the water, miss? – you think she's *in* – ?'

'She may be, though the depth is, I believe, nowhere very great. But what I judge most likely is that she's on the spot from which, the other day, we saw together what I told you.'

'When she pretended not to see – ?'

'With that astounding self-possession! I've always been sure she wanted to go back alone. And now her brother has managed it for her.'

Mrs Grose still stood where she had stopped. 'You suppose they really *talk* of them?'

I could meet this with an assurance! 'They say things that, if we heard them, would simply appal us.'

'And if she *is* there – ?'

'Yes?'

'Then Miss Jessel is?'

'Beyond a doubt. You shall see.'

'Oh, thank you!' my friend cried, planted so firm that, taking it in, I went straight on without her. By the time I reached the pool, however, she was close behind me, and I knew that, whatever, to her apprehension, might befall me, the exposure of sticking to me struck her as her least danger. She exhaled a moan of relief as we at last came in sight of the greater part of the water without a sight of the child. There was no trace of Flora on that nearer side of the bank where my observation of her had been most startling, and none on the opposite edge, where, save for a margin of some twenty yards, a thick copse came down to the water. This expanse, oblong in shape, was so narrow compared to its length that, with its ends out of view, it might have been taken for a scant river. We looked at the empty stretch, and then I felt the suggestion in my friend's eyes. I knew what she meant and I replied with a negative headshake.

'No, no; wait! She has taken the boat.'

My companion stared at the vacant mooring-place and then again across the lake. 'Then where is it?'

'Our not seeing it is the strongest of proofs. She has used it to go over, and then has managed to hide it.'

'All alone – that child?'

'She's not alone, and at such times she's not a child: she's an old, old woman.' I scanned all the visible shore while Mrs Grose took again, into the queer element I offered her, one of her plunges of submission; then I pointed out that the boat might perfectly be in a small refuge formed by one of the recesses of the pool, an indentation masked, for the hither side, by a projection of the bank and by a clump of trees growing close to the water.

'But if the boat's there, where on earth's *she*?' my colleague anxiously asked.

'That's exactly what we must learn.' And I started to walk farther.

'By going all the way round?'

'Certainly, far as it is. It will take us but ten minutes, yet it's far enough to have made the child prefer not to walk. She went straight over.'

'Laws!' cried my friend again; the chain of my logic was ever too strong for her. It dragged her at my heels even now, and when we had got halfway round – a devious tiresome process, on ground much broken and by a path choked with overgrowth – I paused to give her breath. I sustained her with a grateful arm, assuring her that she might hugely help me; and this started us afresh, so that in the course of but few minutes more we reached a point from which we found the boat to be where I had supposed it. It had been intentionally left as much as possible out of sight and was tied to one of the stakes of a fence that came, just there, down to the brink and that had been an assistance to disembarking. I recognised, as I looked at the pair of short, thick oars, quite safely drawn up, the prodigious character of the feat for a little girl; but

I had by this time lived too long among wonders and had panted to too many livelier measures. There was a gate in the fence, through which we passed, and that brought us after a trifling interval more into the open. Then 'There she is!' we both exclaimed at once.

Flora, a short way off, stood before us on the grass and smiled as if her performance had now become complete. The next thing she did, however, was to stoop straight down and pluck – quite as if it were all she was there for – a big, ugly spray of withered fern. I at once felt sure she had just come out of the copse. She waited for us, not herself taking a step, and I was conscious of the rare solemnity with which we presently approached her. She smiled and smiled, and we met; but it was all done in a silence by this time flagrantly ominous. Mrs Grose was the first to break the spell: she threw herself on her knees and, drawing the child to her breast, clasped in a long embrace the little, tender, yielding body. While this dumb convulsion lasted I could only watch it – which I did the more intently when I saw Flora's face peep at me over our companion's shoulder. It was serious now – the flicker had left it; but it strengthened the pang with which I at that moment envied Mrs Grose the simplicity of *her* relation. Still, all this while, nothing more passed between us save that Flora had let her foolish fern again drop to the ground. What she and I had virtually said to each other was that pretexts were useless now. When Mrs Grose finally got up, she kept the child's hand, so that the two were still before me; and the singular reticence of our communion was even more marked in the frank look she addressed me. 'I'll be hanged,' it said, 'if *I'll* speak!'

It was Flora who, gazing all over me in candid

wonder, was the first. She was struck with our bare-headed aspect. 'Why, where are your things?'

'Where yours are, my dear!' I promptly returned.

She had already got back her gaiety and appeared to take this as an answer quite sufficient. 'And where's Miles?' she went on.

There was something in the small valour of it that quite finished me: these three words from her were in a flash like the glitter of a drawn blade, the jostle of the cup that my hand for weeks and weeks had held high and full to the brim and that now, even before speaking, I felt overflow in a deluge. 'I'll tell you if you'll tell *me* – ' I heard myself say, then heard the tremor in which it broke.

'Well, what?'

Mrs Grose's suspense blazed at me, but it was too late now, and I brought the thing out handsomely. 'Where, my pet, is Miss Jessel?'

CHAPTER 20

Just as in the churchyard with Miles, the whole thing was upon us. Much as I had made of the fact that this name had never once, between us, been sounded, the quick smitten glare with which the child's face now received it fairly likened my breach of the silence to the smash of a pane of glass. It added to the interposing cry, as if to stay the blow, that Mrs Grose at the same instant uttered over my violence – the shriek of a creature scared, or rather wounded, which, in turn, within a few seconds, was completed by a gasp of my own. I seized my colleague's arm. 'She's there, she's there!'

Miss Jessel stood before us on the opposite bank exactly as she had stood the other time, and I remember, strangely, as the first feeling now produced in me, my thrill of joy at having brought on a proof. She was there, so I was justified; she was there, so I was neither cruel nor mad. She was there for poor scared Mrs Grose, but she was there most for Flora; and no moment of my monstrous time was perhaps so extraordinary as that in which I consciously threw out to her – with the sense that, pale and ravenous demon as she was, she would catch and understand it – an inarticulate message of gratitude. She rose erect on the spot my friend and I had lately quitted, and there wasn't in all the long reach of her desire an inch of her evil that fell short. This first vividness of vision and emotion were things of a few seconds, during which Mrs Grose's dazed blink across to where I pointed struck me as showing that she too at last saw, just as it carried my own eyes precipitately to the child. The revelation then of the manner in which Flora was affected startled me in truth far more than it would have done to find her also merely agitated, for direct dismay was of course not what I had expected. Prepared and on her guard as our pursuit had actually made her, she would repress every betrayal; and I was therefore at once shaken by my first glimpse of the particular one for which I had not allowed. To see her, without a convulsion of her small pink face, not even feign to glance in the direction of the prodigy I announced, but only, instead of that, turn at *me* an expression of hard, still gravity, an expression absolutely new and unprecedented and that appeared to read and accuse and judge me – this was a stroke that somehow converted the little girl

herself into a figure portentous. I gaped at her coolness even though my certitude of her thoroughly
seeing was never greater than at that instant, and
then, in the immediate need to defend myself, I called
her passionately to witness. 'She's there, you little
unhappy thing – there, there, *there*, and you know it
as well as you know me!' I had said shortly before to
Mrs Grose that she was not at these times a child,
but an old, old woman, and my description of her
couldn't have been more strikingly confirmed than in
the way in which, for all notice of this, she simply
showed me, without an expressional concession or
admission, a countenance of deeper and deeper, of
indeed suddenly quite fixed reprobation. I was by this
time – if I can put the whole thing at all together –
more appalled at what I may properly call her manner
than at anything else, though it was quite simul-
taneously that I became aware of having Mrs Grose
also, and very formidably, to reckon with. My elder
companion, the next moment, at any rate, blotted
out everything but her own flushed face and her loud
shocked protest, a burst of high disapproval. 'What a
dreadful turn, to be sure, miss! Where on earth do
you see anything?'

I could only grasp her more quickly yet, for even
while she spoke the hideous plain presence stood
undimmed and undaunted. It had already lasted a
minute, and it lasted while I continued, seizing my
colleague, quite thrusting her at it and presenting her
to it, to insist with my pointing hand. 'You don't see
her exactly as *we* see? – you mean to say you don't
now – *now*? She's as big as a blazing fire! Only look,
dearest woman, *look* – !' She looked, just as I did, and
gave me, with her deep groan of negation, repulsion,

compassion – the mixture with her pity of her relief at her exemption – a sense, touching to me even then, that she would have backed me up if she had been able. I might well have needed that, for with this hard blow of the proof that her eyes were hopelessly sealed, I felt my own situation horribly crumble, I felt – I *saw* – my livid predecessor press, from her position, on my defeat, and I took the measure, more than all, of what I should have from this instant to deal with in the astounding little attitude of Flora. Into this attitude Mrs Grose immediately and violently entered, breaking, even while there pierced through my sense of ruin a prodigious private triumph, into breathless reassurance.

'She isn't there, little lady, and nobody's there – and you never see nothing, my sweet! How can poor Miss Jessel – when poor Miss Jessel's dead and buried? *We* know, don't we, love?' – and she appealed, blundering in, to the child. 'It's all a mere mistake and a worry and a joke – and we'll go home as fast as we can!'

Our companion, on this, had responded with a strange quick primness of propriety, and they were again, with Mrs Grose on her feet, united, as it were, in shocked opposition to me. Flora continued to fix me with her small mask of disaffection, and even at that minute I prayed God to forgive me for seeming to see that, as she stood there holding tight to our friend's dress, her incomparable childish beauty had suddenly failed, had quite vanished. I've said it already – she was literally, she was hideously hard; she had turned common and almost ugly. 'I don't know what you mean. I see nobody. I see nothing. I never *have*. I think you're cruel. I don't like you!'

Then, after this deliverance, which might have been that of a vulgarly pert little girl in the street, she hugged Mrs Grose more closely and buried in her skirts the dreadful little face. In this position she launched an almost furious wail. 'Take me away, take me away – oh, take me away from *her*!'

'From *me*?' I panted.

'From you – from you!' she cried.

Even Mrs Grose looked across at me dismayed, while I had nothing to do but communicate again with the figure that, on the opposite bank, without a movement, as rigidly still as if catching, beyond the interval, our voices, was as vividly there for my disaster as it was not there for my service. The wretched child had spoken exactly as if she had got from some outside source each of her stabbing little words, and I could therefore, in the full despair of all I had to accept, but sadly shake my head at her. 'If I had ever doubted, all my doubt would at present have gone. I've been living with the miserable truth, and now it has only too much closed round me. Of course I've lost you: I've interfered, and you've seen, under *her* dictation' – with which I faced, over the pool again, our infernal witness – 'the easy and perfect way to meet it. I've done my best, but I've lost you. Goodbye.' For Mrs Grose I had an imperative, an almost frantic 'Go, go!' before which, in infinite distress, but mutely possessed of the little girl and clearly convinced, in spite of her blindness, that something awful had occurred and some collapse engulfed us, she retreated, by the way we had come, as fast as she could move.

Of what first happened when I was left alone I had no subsequent memory. I only knew that at the end of, I suppose, a quarter of an hour, an odorous dampness and roughness, chilling and piercing my trouble, had made me understand that I must have thrown myself, on my face, to the ground and given way to a wildness of grief. I must have lain there long and cried and wailed, for when I raised my head the day was almost done. I got up and looked a moment, through the twilight, at the grey pool and its blank haunted edge, and then I took, back to the house, my dreary and difficult course. When I reached the gate in the fence the boat, to my surprise, was gone, so that I had a fresh reflection to make on Flora's extraordinary command of the situation. She passed that night, by the most tacit and, I should add, were not the word so grotesque a false note, the happiest of arrangements, with Mrs Grose. I saw neither of them on my return, but on the other hand I saw, as by an ambiguous compensation, a great deal of Miles. I saw – I can use no other phrase – so much of him that it fairly measured more than it had ever measured. No evening I had passed at Bly was to have had the portentous quality of this one; in spite of which – and in spite also of the deeper depths of consternation that had opened beneath my feet – there was literally, in the ebbing actual, an extraordinarily sweet sadness. On reaching the house I had never so much as looked for the boy; I had simply gone straight to my room to change what I was wearing and to take in, at a glance, much material testimony to Flora's rupture. Her little belongings had all been removed. When later, by the schoolroom fire, I was served with tea by the usual maid, I indulged, on the article of my other pupil, in no inquiry whatever. He had his freedom now – he might have it to the end! Well, he did have it; and it consisted – in part at least – of his coming in at about eight o'clock and sitting down with me in silence. On the removal of the tea things, I had blown out the candles and drawn my chair closer: I was conscious of a mortal coldness and felt as if I should never again be warm. So when he appeared I was sitting in the glow with my thoughts. He paused a moment by the door as if to look at me; then – as if to share them – came to the other side of the hearth and sank into a chair. We sat there in absolute stillness; yet he wanted, I felt, to be with me.

CHAPTER 21

Before a new day, in my room, had fully broken, my eyes opened to Mrs Grose, who had come to my bedside with worse news. Flora was so markedly feverish that an illness was perhaps at hand; she had passed a night of extreme unrest, a night agitated above all by fears that had for their subject not in the least her former but wholly her present governess. It was not against the possible re-entrance of Miss Jessel on the scene that she protested – it was conspicuously and passionately against mine. I was at once on my feet, and with an immense deal to ask; the more that my friend had discernibly now girded her loins to meet me afresh. This I felt as soon as I had put to her the question of her sense of the child's sincerity as against my own. 'She persists in denying to you that she saw, or has ever seen, anything?'

My visitor's trouble truly was great. 'Ah, miss, it isn't a matter on which I can push her. Yet it isn't either, I must say, as if I much needed to. It has made her, every inch of her, quite old.'

'Oh, I see her perfectly from here. She resents, for all the world like some high little personage, the imputation on her truthfulness and, as it were, her respectability. "Miss Jessel indeed – *she*!" Ah, she's "respectable", the chit! The impression she gave me there yesterday was, I assure you, the very strangest of all; it was quite beyond any of the others. I *did* put my foot in it! She'll never speak to me again.'

Hideous and obscure as it all was, it held Mrs Grose briefly silent; then she granted my point with a frankness which, I made sure, had more behind it. 'I think indeed, miss, she never will. She do have a grand manner about it!'

'And that manner' – I summed it up – 'is practically what's the matter with her now.'

Oh, that manner, I could see in my visitor's face, and not a little else besides! 'She asks me every three minutes if I think you're coming in.'

'I see – I see.' I too, on my side, had so much more than worked it out. 'Has she said to you since yesterday – except to repudiate her familiarity with anything so dreadful – a single other word about Miss Jessel?'

'Not one, miss. And of course, you know,' my friend added, 'I took it from her by the lake that just then and there at least there *was* nobody.'

'Rather! And naturally you take it from her still.'

'I don't contradict her. What else can I do?'

'Nothing in the world! You've the cleverest little person to deal with. They've made them – their two friends, I mean – still cleverer even than nature did; for it was wondrous material to play on! Flora has now her grievance, and she'll work it to the end.'

'Yes, miss; but to *what* end?'

'Why, that of dealing with me to her uncle. She'll make me out to him the lowest creature – !'

I winced at the fair show of the scene in Mrs Grose's face; she looked for a minute as if she sharply saw them together. 'And him who thinks so well of you!'

'He has an odd way – it comes over me now,' I laughed, ' – of proving it! But that doesn't matter. What Flora wants of course is to get rid of me.'

My companion bravely concurred. 'Never again to so much as look at you.'

'So that what you've come to me now for,' I asked, 'is to speed me on my way?' Before she had time to reply, however, I had her in check. 'I've a better idea – the result of my reflections. My going *would* seem the right thing, and on Sunday I was terribly near it. Yet that won't do. It's *you* who must go. You must take Flora.'

My visitor, at this, did speculate. 'But where in the world – ?'

'Away from here. Away from *them*. Away, even most of all, now, from me. Straight to her uncle.'

'Only to tell on you – ?'

'No, not "only"! To leave me, in addition, with my remedy.'

She was still vague. 'And what *is* your remedy?'

'Your loyalty, to begin with. And then Miles's.'

She looked at me hard. 'Do you think he – ?'

'Won't, if he has the chance, turn on me? Yes, I venture still to think it. At all events I want to try. Get off with his sister as soon as possible and leave me with him alone.' I was amazed, myself, at the spirit I had still in reserve, and therefore perhaps a trifle the more disconcerted at the way in which, in spite of this fine example of it, she hesitated. 'There's one thing, of course,' I went on: 'they mustn't, before she goes, see each other for three seconds.' Then it came over me that, in spite of Flora's presumable sequestration from the instant of her return from the pool, it might already be too late. 'Do you mean,' I anxiously asked, 'that they *have* met?'

At this she quite flushed. 'Ah, miss, I'm not such a fool as that! If I've been obliged to leave her three or four times, it has been each time with one of the maids, and at present, though she's alone, she's locked in safe. And yet – and yet!' There were too many things.

'And yet what?'

'Well, are you so sure of the little gentleman?'

'I'm not sure of anything but *you*. But I have, since last evening, a new hope. I think he wants to give me an opening. I do believe that – poor little exquisite wretch! – he wants to speak. Last evening, in the firelight and the silence, he sat with me for two hours as if it were just coming.'

Mrs Grose looked hard through the window at the grey gathering day. 'And did it come?'

'No, though I waited and waited I confess it didn't, and it was without a breach of the silence, or so much as a faint allusion to his sister's condition and absence, that we at last kissed for good-night. All the same,' I continued, 'I can't, if her uncle sees her, consent to his seeing her brother without my having given the boy – and most of all because things have got so bad – a little more time.'

My friend appeared on this ground more reluctant than I could quite understand. 'What do you mean by more time?'

'Well, a day or two – really to bring it out. He'll then be on *my* side – of which you see the importance. If nothing comes, I shall only fail, and you at the worst have helped me by doing on your arrival in town whatever you may have found possible.' So I put it before her, but she continued for a little so lost in other reasons that I came again to her aid. 'Unless indeed,' I wound up, 'you really want *not* to go.'

I could see it, in her face, at last clear itself; she put out her hand to me as a pledge. 'I'll go – I'll go. I'll go this morning.'

I wanted to be very just. 'If you *should* wish still to wait, I'd engage she shouldn't see me.'

'No, no: it's the place itself. She must leave it.' She held me a moment with heavy eyes, then brought out the rest. 'Your idea's the right one. I myself, miss – '

'Well?'

'I can't stay.'

The look she gave me with it made me jump at possibilities. 'You mean that, since yesterday, you *have* seen – ?'

She shook her head with dignity. 'I've *heard* – !'

'Heard?'

'From that child – horrors! There!' she sighed with tragic relief. 'On my honour, miss, she says things – !' But at this evocation she broke down; she dropped with a sudden cry upon my sofa and, as I had seen her do before, gave way to all the anguish of it.

It was in quite another manner that I for my part let myself go. 'Oh, thank God!'

She sprang up again at this, drying her eyes with a groan. ' "Thank God"?'

'It so justifies me!'

'It does that, miss!'

I couldn't have desired more emphasis, but I just waited. 'She's so horrible?'

I saw my colleague scarce knew how to put it. 'Really shocking.'

'And about me?'

'About you, miss – since you must have it. It's beyond everything, for a young lady; and I can't think wherever she must have picked up – '

'The appalling language she applies to me? I can, then!' I broke in with a laugh that was doubtless significant enough.

It only in truth left my friend still more grave. 'Well, perhaps I ought to also – since I've heard some of it before! Yet I can't bear it,' the poor woman went on while with the same movement she glanced, on my dressing-table, at the face of my watch. 'But I must go back.'

I kept her, however. 'Ah, if you can't bear it – !'

'How can I stop with her, you mean? Why, just *for* that: to get her away. Far from this,' she pursued, 'far from *them* – '

'She may be different? She may be free?' I seized her almost with joy. 'Then in spite of yesterday you *believe* – '

'In such doings?' Her simple description of them required, in the light of her expression, to be carried no further, and she gave me the whole thing as she had never done. 'I believe.'

Yes, it was a joy, and we were still shoulder to shoulder: if I might continue sure of that I should care but little what else happened. My support in the presence of disaster would be the same as it had been in my early need of confidence, and if my friend would answer for my honesty, I would answer for all the rest. On the point of taking leave of her, none the less, I was to some extent embarrassed. 'There's one thing of course – it occurs to me – to remember. My letter, giving the alarm, will have reached town before you.'

I now felt still more how she had been beating about the bush and how weary at last it had made her. 'Your letter won't have got there. Your letter never went.'

'What then became of it?'

'Goodness knows! Master Miles – '

'Do you mean *he* took it?' I gasped.

She hung fire, but she overcame her reluctance. 'I mean that I saw yesterday, when I came back with Miss Flora, that it wasn't where you had put it. Later in the evening I had the chance to question Luke, and he declared that he had neither noticed nor touched it.' We could only exchange, on this, one of our deeper mutual soundings, and it was Mrs Grose who first brought up the plumb with an almost elate 'You see!'

'Yes, I see that if Miles took it instead, he probably will have read it and destroyed it.'

'And don't you see anything else?'

I faced her a moment with a sad smile. 'It strikes me that by this time your eyes are open even wider than mine.'

They proved to be so indeed, but she could still almost blush to show it. 'I make out now what he must have done at school.' And she gave, in her simple sharpness, an almost droll disillusioned nod. 'He stole!'

I turned it over – I tried to be more judicial. 'Well – perhaps.'

She looked as if she found me unexpectedly calm. 'He stole *letters*!'

She couldn't know my reasons for a calmness after all pretty shallow; so I showed them off as I might. 'I hope then it was to more purpose than in this case! The note, at all events, that I put on the table yesterday,' I pursued, 'will have given him so scant an advantage – for it contained only the bare demand for an interview – that he's already much ashamed of having gone so far for so little, and that which he had on his mind last evening was precisely the need of confession.' I seemed to myself for the instant to have mastered it, to see it all. 'Leave us, leave us' – I was already, at the door, hurrying her off. 'I'll get it out of him. He'll meet me. He'll confess. If he confesses he's saved. And if he's saved – '

'Then *you* are?' The dear woman kissed me on this, and I took her farewell. 'I'll save you without him!' she cried as she went.

CHAPTER 22

Yet it was when she had got off – and I missed her on the spot – that the great pinch really came. If I had counted on what it would give me to find myself alone with Miles I quickly recognised that it would give me at least a measure. No hour of my stay in fact was so assailed with apprehensions as that of my coming down to learn that the carriage containing Mrs Grose and my younger pupil had already rolled out of the gates. Now I was, I said to myself, face to face with the elements, and for much of the rest of the day, while I fought my weakness, I could consider that I had been supremely rash. It was a tighter place still than I had yet turned round in; all the more that, for the first time, I could see in the aspect of others a confused reflection of the crisis. What had happened naturally caused them all to stare; there was too little of the explained, throw out whatever we might, in the suddenness of my colleague's act. The maids and the men looked blank; the effect of which on my nerves was an aggravation until I saw the necessity of making it a positive aid. It was in short by just clutching the helm that I avoided total wreck; and I dare say that, to bear up at all, I became that morning very grand and very dry. I welcomed the consciousness that I was charged with much to do, and I caused it to be known as well that, left thus to myself, I was quite remarkably firm. I wandered with that manner, for the next hour or two, all over the place and looked, I have no doubt, as if I were ready for any onset. So, for the benefit of whom it might concern, I paraded with a sick heart.

The person it appeared least to concern proved to be, till dinner, little Miles himself. My perambulations had given me meanwhile no glimpse of him, but they had tended to make more public the change taking place in our relation as a consequence of his having at the piano, the day before, kept me, in Flora's interest, so beguiled and befooled. The stamp of publicity had of course been fully given by her confinement and departure, and the change itself was now ushered in by our non-observance of the regular custom of the schoolroom. He had already disappeared when, on my way down, I pushed open his door, and I learned below that he had breakfasted – in the presence of a couple of the maids – with Mrs Grose and his sister.

He had then gone out, as he said, for a stroll; than which nothing, I reflected, could better have expressed his frank view of the abrupt transformation of my office. What he would now permit this office to consist of was yet to be settled: there was at least a queer relief – I mean for myself especially – in the renouncement of one pretension. If so much had sprung to the surface I scarce put it too strongly in saying that what had perhaps sprung highest was the absurdity of our prolonging the fiction that I had anything more to teach him. It sufficiently stuck out that, by tacit little tricks in which even more than myself he carried out the care for my dignity, I had had to appeal to him to let me off straining to meet him on the ground of his true capacity. He had at any rate his freedom now; I was never to touch it again; as I had amply shown, moreover, when, on his joining me in the schoolroom the previous night, I uttered, in reference to the interval just concluded, neither challenge nor hint. I had too much, from this moment, my other ideas. Yet when he at last arrived the difficulty of applying them, the accumulations of my problem, were brought straight home to me by the beautiful little presence on which what had occurred had as yet, for the eye, dropped neither stain nor shadow.

To mark, for the house, the high state I cultivated I decreed that my meals with the boy should be served, as we called it, downstairs; so that I had been awaiting him in the ponderous pomp of the room outside the window of which I had had from Mrs Grose, that first scared Sunday, my flash of something it would scarce have done to call light. Here at present I felt afresh – for I had felt it again and again – how my equilibrium depended on the success of my rigid will, the will to shut my eyes as tight as possible to the truth that what I had to deal with was, revoltingly, against nature. I could only get on at all by taking 'nature' into my confidence and my account, by treating my monstrous ordeal as a push in a direction unusual, of course, and unpleasant, but demanding after all, for a fair front, only another turn of the screw of ordinary human virtue. No attempt, none the less, could well require more tact than just this attempt to supply, one's self, *all* the nature. How could I put even a little of that article into a suppression of reference to what had occurred? How on the other hand could I make a reference without a new plunge into the hideous obscure? Well, a sort of answer, after a time, had come to me, and it was so far confirmed as that I was met, incontestably, by the quickened vision of what was rare in my little companion. It was, indeed, as if he had found even now – as he had so often found at lessons – still some other delicate way to ease me off. Wasn't there light in the fact which, as we shared our solitude, broke out with a specious glitter it had never yet quite worn? – the fact that (opportunity aiding, precious opportunity which had now come) it would be preposterous, with a child so endowed, to forgo the help one might wrest from absolute intelligence? What had his intelligence been given him for but to save him? Mightn't one, to reach his mind, risk the stretch of a stiff arm across his character? It was as if, when we were face to face in the dining-room, he had literally shown me the way. The roast mutton was on the table, and I had dispensed with attendance. Miles, before he sat down, stood a moment with his hands in his pockets and looked at the joint, on which he seemed on the point of passing some humorous judgement. But what he presently produced was: 'I say, my dear, is she really very awfully ill?'

'Little Flora? Not so bad but that she'll presently be better. London will set her up. Bly had ceased to agree with her. Come here and take your mutton.'

He alertly obeyed me, carried the plate carefully to his seat and, when he was established, went on. 'Did Bly disagree with her so terribly all at once?'

'Not so suddenly as you might think. One had seen it coming on.'

'Then why didn't you get her off before?'

'Before what?'

'Before she became too ill to travel.'

I found myself prompt. 'She's *not* too ill to travel: she only might have become so if she had stayed. This was just the moment to seize. The journey will dissipate the influence' – oh, I was grand! – 'and carry it off.'

'I see, I see' – Miles, for that matter, was grand too. He settled to his repast with the charming little 'table manner' that, from the day of his arrival, had relieved me of all grossness of admonition. Whatever he had been expelled from school for, it wasn't for ugly feeding. He was irreproachable, as always, today; but was unmistakably more conscious. He was discernibly trying to take for granted more things than he found, without assistance, quite easy; and he dropped into peaceful silence while he felt his situation. Our meal was of the briefest – mine a vain pretence, and I had the things immediately removed. While this was done, Miles stood again with his hands in his little pockets and his back to me – stood and looked out of the wide window through which, that other day, I had seen what pulled me up. We continued silent while the maid was with us – as silent, it whimsically occurred to me, as some young couple who, on their wedding journey, at the inn, feel shy in the presence of the waiter. He turned round only when the waiter had left us. 'Well – so we're alone!'

CHAPTER 23

'Oh, more or less.' I imagine my smile was pale. 'Not absolutely. We shouldn't like that!' I went on.

'No – I suppose we shouldn't. Of course, we've the others.'

'We've the others – we've, indeed, the others,' I concurred.

'Yet even though we have them,' he returned, still with his hands in his pockets and planted there in front of me, 'they don't much count, do they?'

I made the best of it, but I felt wan. 'It depends on what you call "much"!'

'Yes' – with all accommodation – 'everything depends!' On this, however, he faced to the window again and presently reached it with his vague, restless, cogitating step. He remained there awhile with his forehead against the glass, in contemplation of the stupid shrubs I knew and the dull things of November. I had always my hypocrisy of 'work', behind which I now gained the sofa. Steadying myself with it there as I had repeatedly done at those moments of torment that I have described as the moments of my knowing the children to be given to something from which I was barred, I sufficiently obeyed my habit of being prepared for the worst. But an extraordinary impression dropped on me as I extracted a meaning

THE TURN OF THE SCREW

from the boy's embarrassed back – none other than
the impression that I was not barred now. This
inference grew in a few minutes to sharp intensity
and seemed bound up with the direct perception
that it was positively *he* who was. The frames and
squares of the great window were a kind of image, for
him, of a kind of failure. I felt that I saw him, in any
case, shut in or shut out. He was admirable but not
comfortable: I took it in with a throb of hope. Wasn't
he looking through the haunted pane for something
he couldn't see? – and wasn't it the first time in the
whole business that he had known such a lapse? The
first, the very first: I found it a splendid portent. It
made him anxious, though he watched himself; he
had been anxious all day and, even while in his usual
sweet little manner he sat at table, had needed all his
small strange genius to give it a gloss. When he at last
turned round to meet me it was almost as if this
genius had succumbed. 'Well, I think I'm glad Bly
agrees with *me*!'

'You would certainly seem to have seen, these
twenty-four hours, a good deal more of it than for
some time before. I hope,' I went on bravely, 'that
you've been enjoying yourself.'

'Oh, yes, I've been ever so far; all round about –
miles and miles away. I've never been so free.'

He had really a manner of his own, and I could
only try to keep up with him. 'Well, do you like it?'

He stood there smiling; then at last he put into two
words – 'Do *you*?' – more discrimination than I had
ever heard two words contain. Before I had time to
deal with that, however, he continued as if with the
sense that this was an impertinence to be softened.
'Nothing could be more charming than the way you

take it, for of course if we're alone together now it's you that are alone most. But I hope,' he threw in, 'you don't particularly mind!'

'Having to do with you?' I asked. 'My dear child, how can I help minding? Though I've renounced all claim to your company – you're so beyond me – I at least greatly enjoy it. What else should I stay on for?'

He looked at me more directly, and the expression of his face, graver now, struck me as the most beautiful I had ever found in it. 'You stay on just for *that*?'

'Certainly. I stay on as your friend and from the tremendous interest I take in you till something can be done for you that may be more worth your while. That needn't surprise you.' My voice trembled so that I felt it impossible to suppress the shake. 'Don't you remember how I told you, when I came and sat on your bed the night of the storm, that there was nothing in the world I wouldn't do for you?'

'Yes, yes!' He, on his side, more and more visibly nervous, had a tone to master; but he was so much more successful than I that, laughing out through his gravity, he could pretend we were pleasantly jesting. 'Only that, I think, was to get me to do something for *you*!'

'It was partly to get you to do something,' I conceded. 'But, you know, you didn't do it.'

'Oh, yes,' he said with the brightest superficial eagerness, 'you wanted me to tell you something.'

'That's it. Out, straight out. What you have on your mind, you know.'

'Ah, then is *that* what you've stayed over for?'

He spoke with a gaiety through which I could still catch the finest little quiver of resentful passion; but I can't begin to express the effect upon me of an implication of surrender even so faint. It was as if what I had yearned for had come at last only to astonish me. 'Well, yes – I may as well make a clean breast of it. It was precisely for that.'

He waited so long that I supposed it for the purpose of repudiating the assumption on which my action had been founded; but what he finally said was: 'Do you mean now – here?'

'There couldn't be a better place or time.' He looked round him uneasily, and I had the rare – oh, the queer! – impression of the very first symptom I had seen in him of the approach of immediate fear. It was as if he were suddenly afraid of me – which struck me, indeed, as perhaps the best thing to make him. Yet in the very pang of the effort I felt it vain to try sternness, and I heard myself the next instant so gentle as to be almost grotesque. 'You want so to go out again?'

'Awfully!' He smiled at me heroically, and the touching little bravery of it was enhanced by his actually flushing with pain. He had picked up his hat, which he had brought in, and stood twirling it in a way that gave me, even as I was just nearly reaching port, a perverse horror of what I was doing. To do it in *any* way was an act of violence, for what did it consist of but the obtrusion of the idea of grossness and guilt on a small, helpless creature who had been for me a revelation of the possibilities of beautiful intercourse? Wasn't it base to create for a being so exquisite a mere alien awkwardness? I suppose I now read into our situation a clearness it couldn't have had at the time, for I seem to see our poor eyes already lighted with some spark of a prevision of the anguish that was to come. So we circled about with terrors and scruples, fighters not daring to close. But it was for each other we feared! That kept us a little longer suspended and unbruised. 'I'll tell you everything,' Miles said – 'I mean I'll tell you anything you like. You'll stay on with me, and we shall both be all right, and I *will* tell you – I *will*. But not now.'

'Why not now?'

My resistance turned him from me and kept him once more at his window in a silence during which, between us, you might have heard a pin drop. Then he was before me again with the air of a person for whom, outside, someone who had frankly to be reckoned with was waiting. 'I have to see Luke.'

I had not yet reduced him to quite so vulgar a lie, and I felt proportionately ashamed. But, horrible as it was, his lies made up my truth. I achieved thoughtfully a few loops of my knitting.

'Well, then go to Luke, and I'll wait for what you promise. Only in return for that satisfy, before you leave me, one very much smaller request.'

He looked as if he felt he had succeeded enough to be able still a little to bargain. 'Very much smaller – ?'

'Yes, a mere fraction of the whole. Tell me' – oh, my work preoccupied me, and I was offhand! – 'if, yesterday afternoon, from the table in the hall, you took, you know, my letter.'

CHAPTER 24

My grasp of how he received this suffered for a minute from something that I can describe only as a fierce split of my attention – a stroke that at first, as I sprang straight up, reduced me to the mere blind movement of getting hold of him, drawing him close and, while I just fell for support against the nearest piece of furniture, instinctively keeping him with his back to the window. The appearance was full upon us that I had already had to deal with here: Peter Quint had come into view like a sentinel before a prison. The next thing I saw was that, from outside, he had reached the window, and then I knew that, close to the glass and glaring in through it, he offered once more to the room his white face of damnation. It represents but grossly what took place within me at the sight to say that on the second my decision was made; yet I believe that no woman so overwhelmed ever in so short a time recovered her command of the act. It came to me in the very horror of the immediate presence that the act would be, seeing and facing what I saw and faced, to keep the boy himself unaware. The inspiration – I can call it by no other name – was that I felt how voluntarily, how transcendently, I *might*. It was like fighting with a demon for a human soul, and when I had fairly so appraised it I saw how the human soul – held out, in the tremor of my hands, at arms' length – had a perfect dew of sweat on a lovely childish forehead. The face that was close to mine was as white as the face against the glass, and out of it presently came a sound, not low nor weak, but as if from much farther away, that I drank like a waft of fragrance.

'Yes – I took it.'

At this, with a moan of joy, I enfolded, I drew him close; and while I held him to my breast, where I could feel in the sudden fever of his little body the tremendous pulse of his little heart, I kept my eyes on the thing at the window and saw it move and shift its posture. I have likened it to a sentinel, but its slow wheel, for a moment, was rather the prowl of a baffled beast. My present quickened courage, however, was such that, not too much to let it through, I had to shade, as it were, my flame. Meanwhile the glare of the face was again at the window, the scoundrel fixed as if to watch and wait. It was the very confidence that I might now defy him, as well as the positive certitude, by this time, of the child's unconsciousness, that made me go on. 'What did you take it for?'

'To see what you said about me.'

'You opened the letter?'

'I opened it.'

My eyes were now, as I held him off a little again, on Miles's own face, in which the collapse of mockery showed me how complete was the ravage of uneasiness. What was prodigious was that at last, by my success, his sense was sealed and his communication stopped: he knew that he was in presence, but knew not of what, and knew still less that I also was and that I did know. And what did this strain of trouble matter when my eyes went back to the window only to see that the air was clear again and – by my personal triumph – the influence quenched? There was nothing there. I felt that the cause was mine and that I should surely get *all*. 'And you found nothing!' – I let my elation out.

He gave me the most mournful, thoughtful little headshake. 'Nothing.'

'Nothing, nothing!' I almost shouted in my joy.

'Nothing, nothing,' he sadly repeated.

I kissed his forehead; it was drenched. 'So what have you done with it?'

'I've burnt it.'

'Burnt it?' It was now or never. 'Is that what you did at school?'

Oh, what this brought up! 'At school?'

'Did you take letters? – or other things?'

'Other things?' He appeared now to be thinking of something far off and that reached him only through the pressure of his anxiety. Yet it did reach him. 'Did I *steal*?'

I felt myself redden to the roots of my hair as well as wonder if it were more strange to put to a gentleman such a question or to see him take it with allowances that gave the very distance of his fall in the world. 'Was it for that you mightn't go back?'

The only thing he felt was rather a dreary little surprise. 'Did you know I mightn't go back?'

'I know everything.'

He gave me at this the longest and strangest look. 'Everything?'

'Everything. Therefore *did* you – ?' But I couldn't say it again.

Miles could, very simply. 'No. I didn't steal.'

My face must have shown him I believed him utterly; yet my hands – but it was for pure tenderness – shook him as if to ask him why, if it was all for nothing, he had condemned me to months of torment. 'What then did you do?'

He looked in vague pain all round the top of the room and drew his breath, two or three times over, as if with difficulty. He might have been standing at the bottom of the sea and raising his eyes to some faint green twilight. 'Well – I said things.'

'Only that?'

'They thought it was enough!'

'To turn you out for?'

Never, truly, had a person 'turned out' shown so little to explain it as this little person! He appeared to weigh my question, but in a manner quite detached and almost helpless. 'Well, I suppose I oughtn't.'

'But to whom did you say them?'

He evidently tried to remember, but it dropped – he had lost it. 'I don't know!'

He almost smiled at me in the desolation of his surrender, which was, indeed, practically, by this time, so complete that I ought to have left it there. But I was infatuated – I was blind with victory though even then the very effect that was to have brought him so much nearer was already that of added separation. 'Was it to everyone?' I asked.

'No; it was only to – ' But he gave a sick little headshake. 'I don't remember their names.'

'Were they then so many?'

'No – only a few. Those I liked.'

Those he liked? I seemed to float not into clearness, but into a darker obscure, and within a minute there had come to me out of my very pity the appalling alarm of his being perhaps innocent. It was for the instant confounding and bottomless, for if he *were* innocent what then on earth was *I*? Paralysed, while it lasted, by the mere brush of the question, I let him go a little, so that, with a deep-drawn sigh, he turned away from me again; which, as he faced towards the clear window, I suffered, feeling that I had nothing now there to keep him from. 'And did they repeat what you said?' I went on after a moment.

He was soon at some distance from me, still breathing hard and again with the air, though now without anger for it, of being confined against his will. Once more, as he had done before, he looked up at the dim day as if, of what had hitherto sustained him, nothing was left but an unspeakable anxiety. 'Oh, yes,' he nevertheless replied – 'they must have repeated them. To those *they* liked,' he added.

There was somehow less of it than I had expected; but I turned it over. 'And these things came round – ?'

'To the masters? Oh, yes!' he answered very simply. 'But I didn't know they'd tell.'

'The masters? They didn't – they've never told. That's why I ask you.'

He turned to me again his little beautiful fevered face. 'Yes, it was too bad.'

'Too bad?'

'What I suppose I sometimes said. To write home.'

I can't name the exquisite pathos of the contradiction given to such a speech by such a speaker; I only know that the next instant I heard myself throw off with homely force: 'Stuff and nonsense!' But the next after that I must have sounded stern enough. 'What *were* these things?'

My sternness was all for his judge, his executioner; yet it made him avert himself again, and that movement made *me*, with a single bound and an irrepressible cry, spring straight upon him. For there again, against the glass, as if to blight his confession and stay his answer, was the hideous author of our woe – the white face of damnation. I felt a sick swim at the drop of my victory and all the return of my battle, so that the wildness of my veritable leap only served as a great betrayal. I saw him, from the midst of my act, meet it with a divination, and on the perception that even now he only guessed, and that the window was still to his own eyes free, I let the impulse flame up to convert the climax of his dismay into the very proof of his liberation. 'No more, no more, no more!' I shrieked to my visitant as I tried to press him against me.

'Is she *here*?' Miles panted as he caught with his sealed eyes the direction of my words. Then as his strange 'she' staggered me and, with a gasp, I echoed it, 'Miss Jessel, Miss Jessel!' he with sudden fury gave me back.

I seized, stupefied, his supposition – some sequel to what we had done to Flora, but this made me only want to show him that it was better still than that. 'It's not Miss Jessel! But it's at the window – straight before us. It's *there* – the coward horror, there for the last time!'

At this, after a second in which his head made the movement of a baffled dog's on a scent and then gave a frantic little shake for air and light, he was at me in a white rage, bewildered, glaring vainly over the place and missing wholly, though it now, to my sense, filled the room like the taste of poison, the wide over-whelming presence. 'It's *he*?'

I was so determined to have all my proof that I dashed into ice to challenge him. 'Whom do you mean by "he"?'

'Peter Quint – you devil!' His face gave again, round the room, its convulsed supplication. '*Where*?'

They are in my ears still, his supreme surrender of the name and his tribute to my devotion. 'What does he matter now, my own? – what will he *ever* matter? *I* have you,' I launched at the beast, 'but he has lost you for ever!' Then, for the demonstration of my work, 'There, *there*!' I said to Miles.

But he had already jerked straight round, stared, glared again, and seen but the quiet day. With the stroke of the loss I was so proud of he uttered the cry of a creature hurled over an abyss, and the grasp with which I recovered him might have been that of catching him in his fall. I caught him, yes, I held him – it may be imagined with what a passion; but at the end of a minute I began to feel what it truly was that I held. We were alone with the quiet day, and his little heart, dispossessed, had stopped.

OWEN WINGRAVE

CHAPTER I

'Upon my honour you must be off your head!' cried Spencer Coyle as the young man, with a white face, stood there panting a little and repeating, 'Really I've quite decided,' and, 'I assure you I've thought it all out.' They were both pale, but Owen Wingrave smiled in a manner exasperating to his supervisor, who however still discriminated sufficiently to feel his grimace – it was like an irrelevant leer – the result of extreme and conceivable nervousness.

'It was certainly a mistake to have gone so far; but that's exactly why it strikes me I mustn't go further,' poor Owen said, waiting mechanically, almost humbly – he wished not to swagger, and indeed had nothing to swagger about – and carrying through the window to the stupid opposite houses the dry glitter of his eyes.

'I'm unspeakably disgusted. You've made me dreadfully ill' – and Mr Coyle looked in truth thoroughly upset.

'I'm very sorry. It was the fear of the effect on you that kept me from speaking sooner.'

'You should have spoken three months ago. Don't you know your mind from one day to the other?' the elder of the pair demanded.

The young man for a moment held himself: then he quavered his plea. 'You're very angry with me and I expected it. I'm awfully obliged to you for all you've done for me. I'll do anything else for you in return, but I can't do that. Everyone else will let me have it of

155

course. I'm prepared for that – I'm prepared for everything. It's what has taken the time: to be sure I was prepared. I think it's your displeasure I feel most and regret most. But little by little you'll get over it,' Owen wound up.

'*You'll* get over it rather faster, I suppose!' the other satirically exclaimed. He was quite as agitated as his young friend, and they were evidently in no condition to prolong an encounter in which each drew blood. Mr Coyle was a professional 'coach'; he prepared aspirants for the army, taking only three or four at a time, to whom he applied the irresistible stimulus the possession of which was both his secret and his fortune. He hadn't a great establishment; he would have said himself that it was not a wholesale business. Neither his system, his health nor his temper could have concorded with numbers; so he weighed and measured his pupils and turned away more applicants than he passed. He was an artist in his line, caring only for picked subjects and capable of sacrifices almost passionate for the individual. He liked ardent young men – there were types of facility and kinds of capacity to which he was indifferent – and he had taken a particular fancy to Owen Wingrave. This young man's particular shade of ability, to say nothing of his whole personality, almost cast a spell and at any rate worked a charm. Mr Coyle's candidates usually did wonders, and he might have sent up a multitude. He was a person exactly of the stature of the great Napoleon, with a certain flicker of genius in his light blue eye: it had been said of him that he looked like a concert-giving pianist. The tone of his favourite pupil now expressed, without intention indeed, a superior wisdom that irritated him. He hadn't at all suffered before from Wingrave's high opinion of himself, which had seemed justified by remarkable parts; but today, of a sudden, it struck him as intolerable. He cut short the discussion, declining absolutely to regard their relations as terminated, and remarked to his pupil that he had better go off somewhere – down to Eastbourne, say: the sea would bring him round – and take a few days to find his feet and come to his senses. He could afford the time, he was so well up: when Spencer Coyle remembered how well up he was he could have boxed his ears. The tall athletic young man wasn't physically a subject for simplified reasoning; but a troubled gentleness in his handsome face, the index of compunction mixed with resolution, virtually signified that if it could have done any good he would have turned both cheeks. He evidently didn't pretend that his wisdom was superior; he only presented it as his own. It was his own career after all that was in question. He couldn't refuse to go through the form of trying Eastbourne or at least of holding his tongue, though there was that in his manner which implied that if he should do so it would be really to give Mr Coyle a chance to recuperate. He didn't feel a bit overworked, but there was nothing more natural than that, with their tremendous pressure, Mr Coyle should be. Mr Coyle's own intellect would derive an advantage from his pupil's holiday. Mr Coyle saw what he meant, but controlled himself; he only demanded, as his right, a truce of three days. Owen granted it, though as fostering sad illusions this went visibly against his conscience; but before they separated the famous crammer remarked: 'All the same, I feel I ought to see someone. I think you mentioned to me that your aunt had come to town?'

'Oh yes – she's in Baker Street. Do go and see her,' the boy said for comfort.

His tutor sharply eyed him. 'Have you broached this folly to her?'

'Not yet – to no one. I thought it right to speak to you first.'

'Oh what you "think right"!' cried Spencer Coyle, outraged by his young friend's standards. He added that he would probably call on Miss Wingrave; after which the recreant youth got out of the house.

The latter didn't, none the less, start at once for Eastbourne; he only directed his steps to Kensington Gardens, from which Mr Coyle's desirable residence – he was terribly expensive and had a big house – was not far removed. The famous coach 'put up' his pupils, and Owen had mentioned to the butler that he would be back to dinner. The spring day was warm to his young blood, and he had a book in his pocket which, when he had passed into the Gardens and, after a short stroll, dropped into a chair, he took out with the slow soft sigh that finally ushers in a pleasure postponed. He stretched his long legs and began to read it; it was a volume of Goethe's poems. He had been for days in a state of the highest tension, and now that the cord had snapped the relief was proportionate; only it was characteristic of him that this deliverance should take the form of an intellectual pleasure. If he had thrown up the probability of a magnificent career it wasn't to dawdle along Bond Street nor parade his indifference in the window of a club. At any rate, he had in a few moments forgotten everything – the tremendous pressure, Mr Coyle's disappointment and even his formidable aunt in Baker Street. If these watchers had overtaken him there would surely have been some excuse for their exasperation. There was no doubt he was perverse, for his very choice of a pastime only showed how he had got up his German.

'What the devil's the matter with him, do *you* know?' Spencer Coyle asked that afternoon of young Lechmere, who had never before observed the head of the establishment to set a fellow such an example of bad language. Young Lechmere was not only Wingrave's fellow pupil, he was supposed to be his intimate, indeed quite his best friend, and had unconsciously performed for Mr Coyle the office of making the promise of his great gifts more vivid by contrast. He was short and sturdy and as a general thing uninspired, and Mr Coyle, who found no amusement in believing in him, had never thought him less exciting than as he stared now out of a face from which you could no more guess whether he had caught an idea than you could judge of your dinner by looking at a dish-cover. Young Lechmere concealed such achievements as if they had been youthful indiscretions. At any rate, he could evidently conceive no reason why it should be thought there was anything more than usual the matter with the companion of his studies; so Mr Coyle had to continue: 'He declines to go up. He chucks the whole shop!'

The first thing that struck young Lechmere in the case was the freshness, as of a forgotten vernacular, it had imparted to the governor's vocabulary. 'He doesn't want to go to Sandhurst?'

'He doesn't want to go anywhere. He gives up the army altogether. He objects,' said Mr Coyle in a tone that made young Lechmere almost hold his breath, 'to the military profession.'

'Why, it has been the profession of all his family!'

'Their profession? It has been their religion! Do you know Miss Wingrave?'

'Oh yes. Isn't she awful?' young Lechmere candidly ejaculated.

His instructor demurred. 'She's formidable, if you mean that, and it's right she should be; because somehow in her very person, good maiden lady as she is, she represents the might, she represents the traditions and the exploits, of the British army. She represents the expansive property of the English name. I think his family can be trusted to come down on him, but every influence should be set in motion. I want to know what yours is. Can *you* do anything in the matter?'

'I can try a couple of rounds with him,' said young Lechmere reflectively. 'But he knows a fearful lot. He has the most extraordinary ideas.'

'Then he has told you some of them – he has taken you into his confidence?'

'I've heard him jaw by the yard,' smiled the honest youth. 'He has told me he despises it.'

'What *is* it he despises? I can't make out.'

The most consecutive of Mr Coyle's nurslings considered a moment, as if he were conscious of a responsibility. 'Why I think just soldiering, don't you know? He says we take the wrong view of it.'

'He oughtn't to talk to *you* that way. It's corrupting the youth of Athens. It's sowing sedition.'

'Oh I'm all right!' said young Lechmere. 'And he never told me he meant to chuck it. I always thought he meant to see it through, simply because he had to. He'll argue on any side you like. He can talk your head off – I will say *that* for him. But it's a tremendous pity – I'm sure he'd have a big career.'

'Tell him so then; plead with him; struggle with him – for God's sake.'

'I'll do what I can – I'll tell him it's a regular shame.'

'Yes, strike *that* note – insist on the disgrace of it.'

The young man gave Mr Coyle a queer look. 'I'm sure he wouldn't do anything dishonourable.'

'Well – it won't look right. He must be made to feel *that* – work it up. Give him a comrade's point of view – that of a brother-in-arms.'

'That's what I thought we were going to be!' young Lechmere mused romantically, much uplifted by the nature of the mission imposed on him. 'He's an awfully good sort.'

'No one will think so if he backs out!' said Spencer Coyle.

'Well, they mustn't say it to *me*!' his pupil rejoined with a flush.

Mr Coyle debated, noting his tone and aware that in the perversity of things, though this young man was a born soldier, no excitement would ever attach to *his* alternatives save perhaps on the part of the nice girl to whom at an early day he was sure to be placidly united. 'Do you like him very much – do you believe in him?'

Young Lechmere's life in these days was spent in answering terrible questions, but he had never been put through so straight a lot as these. 'Believe in him? Rather!'

'Then *save* him!'

The poor boy was puzzled, as if it were forced upon him by this intensity that there was more in such an appeal than could appear on the surface; and he doubtless felt that he was but apprehending a complex situation when after another moment, with his hands in his pockets, he replied hopefully but not pompously: 'I dare say I can bring him round!'

CHAPTER 2

Before seeing young Lechmere Mr Coyle had determined to telegraph an enquiry to Miss Wingrave. He had prepaid the answer, which, being promptly put into his hand, brought the interview we have just related to a close. He immediately drove off to Baker Street, where the lady had said she awaited him, and five minutes after he got there, as he sat with Owen Wingrave's remarkable aunt, he repeated several times over, in his angry sadness and with the infallibility of his experience: 'He's so intelligent – he's so intelligent!' He had declared it had been a luxury to put such a fellow through.

'Of course he's intelligent; what else could he be? We've never, that I know of, had but *one* idiot in the family!' said Jane Wingrave. This was an allusion that Mr Coyle could understand, and it brought home to him another of the reasons for the disappointment, the humiliation as it were, of the good people at Paramore, at the same time that it gave an example of the conscientious coarseness he had on former occasions observed in his hostess. Poor Philip Wingrave, her late brother's eldest son, was literally imbecile and banished from view; deformed, unsocial, irretrievable, he had been relegated to a private asylum and had become among the friends of the family only a little hushed lugubrious legend. All the hopes of the house, picturesque Paramore, now unintermittently old Sir Philip's rather melancholy home – his infirmities would keep him there to the last – were therefore gathered on the second boy's head, which nature, as if in compunction for her previous botch, had, in addition to making it strikingly handsome, filled with a marked and general readiness. These two had been the only children of the old man's only son, who, like so many of his ancestors, had given up a gallant young life to the service of his country. Owen Wingrave the elder had received his death-cut, in close quarters, from an Afghan sabre; the blow had come crashing across his skull. His wife, at that time in India, was about to give birth to her third child; and when the event took place, in darkness and anguish, the baby came lifeless into the world and the mother sank under the multiplication of her woes. The second of the little boys in England, who was at Paramore with his grandfather, became the peculiar charge of his aunt, the only unmarried one, and during the interesting Sunday that, by urgent invitation, Spencer Coyle, busy as he was, had, after consenting to put Owen through, spent under that roof, the celebrated crammer received a vivid impression of the influence exerted at least in intention by Miss Wingrave. Indeed the picture of this short visit remained with the observant little man a curious one – the vision of an impoverished Jacobean house, shabby and remarkably 'creepy', but full of character still and full of felicity as a setting for the distinguished figure of the peaceful old soldier. Sir Philip Wingrave, a relic rather than a celebrity, was a small brown erect octogenarian, with smouldering eyes and a studied courtesy. He liked to do the diminished honours of his house, but even when with a shaky hand he lighted a bedroom candle for a deprecating guest, it was impossible not to feel him, beneath the surface, a merciless old man of blood. The eye of the imagination could glance back into his crowded Eastern past – back at episodes in which his scrupulous forms would only have made him more terrible. He had his legend – and oh there were stories about him!

Mr Coyle remembered also two other figures – a faded inoffensive Mrs Julian, domesticated there by a system of frequent visits as the widow of an officer and a particular friend of Miss Wingrave, and a remarkably clever little girl of eighteen, who was this lady's daughter and who struck the speculative visitor as already formed for other relations. She was very impertinent to Owen, and in the course of a long walk that he had taken with the young man and the effect of which, in much talk, had been to clinch his high opinion of him, he had learned – for Owen chattered confidentially – that Mrs Julian was the sister of a very gallant gentleman, Captain Hume-Walker of the Artillery, who had fallen in the Indian Mutiny and between whom and Miss Wingrave (it had been that lady's one known concession) a passage of some delicacy, taking a tragic turn, was believed to have been enacted. They had been engaged to be married, but she had given way to the jealousy of her nature – had broken with him and sent him off to his fate, which had been horrible. A passionate sense of having wronged him, a hard eternal remorse had thereupon taken possession of her, and when his poor sister, linked also to a soldier, had by a still heavier blow been left almost without resources, she had devoted herself grimly to a long expiation. She had sought comfort in taking Mrs

Julian to live much of the time at Paramore, where she became an unremunerated though not uncriticised housekeeper, and Spencer Coyle rather fancied it a part of this comfort that she could at leisure trample on her. The impression of Jane Wingrave was not the faintest he had gathered on that intensifying Sunday – an occasion singularly tinged for him with the sense of bereavement and mourning and memory, of names never mentioned, of the faraway plaint of widows and the echoes of battles and bad news. It was all military indeed, and Mr Coyle was made to shudder a little at the profession of which he helped to open the door to otherwise harmless young men. Miss Wingrave might moreover have made such a bad conscience worse – so cold and clear a good one looked at him out of her hard fine eyes and trumpeted in her sonorous voice.

She was a high distinguished person, angular but not awkward, with a large forehead and abundant black hair arranged like that of a woman conceiving, perhaps excusably, of her head as 'noble', and today irregularly streaked with white. If however she represented for our troubled friend the genius of a military race, it was not that she had the step of a grenadier or the vocabulary of a camp-follower; it was only that such sympathies were vividly implied in the general fact to which her very presence and each of her actions and glances and tones were a constant and direct allusion – the paramount valour of her family. If she was military it was because she sprang from a military house and because she wouldn't for the world have been anything but what the Wingraves had been. She was almost vulgar about her ancestors, and if one had been tempted to quarrel with her one would have found a fair pretext in her defective sense of proportion. This temptation however said nothing to Spencer Coyle, for whom, as a strong character revealing itself in colour and sound, she was almost a 'treat' and who was glad to regard her as a force exerted on his own side. He wished her nephew had more of her narrowness instead of being almost cursed with the tendency to look at things in their relations. He wondered why when she came up to town she always resorted to Baker Street for lodgings. He had never known nor heard of Baker Street as a residence – he associated it only with bazaars and photographers. He divined in her a rigid indifference to everything that was not the passion of her life. Nothing really mattered to her but that, and she would have occupied apartments in Whitechapel if they had been an item in her tactics. She had received her visitor in a large cold faded room, furnished with slippery seats and decorated with alabaster vases and wax-flowers. The only little personal comfort for which she appeared to have looked out was a fat catalogue of the Army and Navy Stores, which reposed on a vast desolate table-cover of false blue. Her clear forehead – it was like a porcelain slate, a receptacle for addresses and sums – had flushed when her nephew's crammer told her the extraordinary news; but he saw she was fortunately more angry than frightened. She had essentially, she would always have, too little imagination for fear, and the healthy habit moreover of facing everything had taught her that the occasion usually found her a quantity to reckon with. He saw that her only present fear could have been that of the failure to prevent her nephew's showing publicly for an ass, or for worse, and that to such an apprehension as this she was in fact inaccessible. Practically, too, she was not troubled by surprise; she recognised none of the futile, none of the subtle sentiments. If Owen had for an hour made a fool of himself she was angry; disconcerted as she would have been on learning that he had confessed to debts or fallen in love with a low girl. But there remained in any annoyance the saving fact that no one could make a fool of *her*.

'I don't know when I've taken such an interest in a young man – I think I've never done it since I began to handle them,' Mr Coyle said. 'I like him, I believe in him. It's been a delight to see how he was going.'

'Oh I know how they go!' Miss Wingrave threw back her head with an air as acquainted as if a headlong array of the generations had flashed before her with a rattle of their scabbards and spurs. Spencer Coyle recognised the intimation that she had nothing to learn from anybody about the natural carriage of a Wingrave, and he even felt convicted by her next words of being, in her eyes, with the troubled story of his check, his weak complaint of his pupil, rather a poor creature. 'If you like him,' she exclaimed, 'for mercy's sake keep him quiet!' Mr Coyle began to explain to her that this was less easy than she appeared to imagine; but it came home to him that she really grasped little of what he said. The more he insisted that the boy had a kind of intellectual independence, the more this struck her as a conclusive proof that her nephew was a Wingrave and a soldier. It was not till he mentioned to her that Owen had spoken of the profession of arms as of something that would be 'beneath' him, it was not till her attention was

arrested by this intenser light on the complexity of
the problem, that she broke out after a moment's
stupefied reflection: 'Send him to see me at once!'

'That's exactly what I wanted to ask your leave to
do. But I've wanted also to prepare you for the worst,
to make you understand that he strikes me as really
obstinate, and to suggest to you that the most powerful arguments at your command – especially if you
should be able to put your hand on some intensely
practical one – will be none too effective.'

'I think I've got a powerful argument' – and Miss
Wingrave looked hard at her visitor. He didn't know
in the least what this engine might be, but he begged
her to drag it without delay into the field. He
promised their young man should come to Baker
Street that evening, mentioning however that he had
already urged him to spend a couple of the very next
days at Eastbourne. This led Jane Wingrave to
enquire with surprise what virtue there might be in
that expensive remedy, and to reply with decision
when he had said 'The virtue of a little rest, a little
change, a little relief to overwrought nerves,' 'Ah
don't coddle him – he's costing us a great deal of
money! I'll talk to him and I'll take him down to
Paramore; he'll be dealt with there, and I'll send him
back to you straightened out.'

Spencer Coyle hailed this pledge superficially with
satisfaction, but before he quitted the strenuous lady
he knew he had really taken on a new anxiety – a
restlessness that made him say to himself, groaning
inwardly: 'Oh she *is* a grenadier at bottom, and
she'll have no tact. I don't know what her powerful
argument is; I'm only afraid she'll be stupid and make
him worse. The old man's better – *he's* capable of

tact, though he's not quite an extinct volcano. Owen will probably put him in a rage. In short, it's a difficulty that the boy's the best of them.'

He felt afresh that evening at dinner that the boy was the best of them. Young Wingrave – who, he was pleased to observe, had not yet proceeded to the seaside – appeared at the repast as usual, looking inevitably a little self-conscious, but not too original for Bayswater. He talked very naturally to Mrs Coyle, who had thought him from the first the most beautiful young man they had ever received; so that the person most ill at ease was poor Lechmere, who took great trouble, as if from the deepest delicacy, not to meet the eye of his misguided mate. Spencer Coyle however paid the price of his own profundity in feeling more and more worried; he could so easily see that there were all sorts of things in his young friend that the people of Paramore wouldn't understand. He began even already to react against the notion of his being harassed – to reflect that after all he had a right to his ideas – to remember that he was of a substance too fine to be handled with blunt fingers. It was in this way that the ardent little crammer, with his whimsical perceptions and complicated sympathies, was generally condemned not to settle down comfortably either to his displeasures or to his enthusiasms. His love of the real truth never gave him a chance to enjoy them. He mentioned to Wingrave after dinner the propriety of an immediate visit to Baker Street, and the young man, looking 'queer', as he thought – that is smiling again with the perverse high spirit in a wrong cause that he had shown in their recent interview – went off to face the ordeal. Spencer Coyle was sure he was scared – he was afraid of his aunt;

but somehow this didn't strike him as a sign of pusillanimity. *He* should have been scared, he was well aware, in the poor boy's place, and the sight of his pupil marching up to the battery in spite of his terrors was a positive suggestion of the temperament of the soldier. Many a plucky youth would have funked this special exposure.

'He *has* got ideas!' young Lechmere broke out to his instructor after his comrade had quitted the house. He was bewildered and rather rueful – he had an emotion to work off. He had before dinner gone straight at his friend, as Mr Coyle had requested, and had elicited from him that his scruples were founded on an overwhelming conviction of the stupidity – the 'crass barbarism' he called it – of war. His great complaint was that people hadn't invented anything cleverer, and he was determined to show, the only way he could, that *he* wasn't so dull a brute.

'And he thinks all the great generals ought to have been shot, and that Napoleon Bonaparte in particular, the greatest, was a scoundrel, a criminal, a monster for whom language has no adequate name!' Mr Coyle rejoined, completing young Lechmere's picture. 'He favoured you, I see, with exactly the same pearls of wisdom that he produced for me. But I want to know what *you* said.'

'I said they were awful rot!' Young Lechmere spoke with emphasis and was slightly surprised to hear Mr Coyle laugh, out of tune, at this just declaration, and then after a moment continue: 'It's all very curious – I dare say there's something in it. But it's a pity!'

'He told me when it was that the question began to strike him in that light. Four or five years ago, when he did a lot of reading about all the great swells and their campaigns – Hannibal and Julius Caesar, Marlborough and Frederick and Bonaparte. He *has* done a lot of reading, and he says it opened his eyes. He says that a wave of disgust rolled over him. He talked about the "immeasurable misery" of wars, and asked me why nations don't tear to pieces the governments, the rulers that go in for them. He hates poor old Bonaparte worst of all.'

'Well, poor old Bonaparte *was* a scoundrel. He was a frightful ruffian,' Mr Coyle unexpectedly declared. 'But I suppose you didn't admit that.'

'Oh I dare say he was objectionable, and I'm very glad we laid him on his back. But the point I made to Wingrave was that his own behaviour would excite no end of remark.' And young Lechmere hung back but an instant before adding: 'I told him he must be prepared for the worst.'

'Of course he asked you what you meant by the "worst",' said Spencer Coyle.

'Yes, he asked me that, and do you know what I said? I said people would call his conscientious scruples and his wave of disgust a mere pretext. Then he asked, "A pretext for what?"'

'Ah he rather had you there!' Mr Coyle returned with a small laugh that was mystifying to his pupil.

'Not a bit – for I told him.'

'What did you tell him?'

Once more, for a few seconds, with his conscious eyes in his instructor's, the young man delayed. 'Why what we spoke of a few hours ago. The appearance he'd present of not having – ' The honest youth faltered afresh, but brought it out: 'The military temperament, don't you know? But do you know how he cheeked us on that?' young Lechmere went on.

'Damn the military temperament!' the crammer promptly replied.

Young Lechmere stared. Mr Coyle's tone left him uncertain if he were attributing the phrase to Wingrave or uttering his own opinion, but he exclaimed: 'Those were exactly his words!'

'He doesn't care,' said Mr Coyle.

'Perhaps not. But it isn't fair for him to abuse *us* fellows. I told him it's the finest temperament in the world, and that there's nothing so splendid as pluck and heroism.'

'Ah! There you had *him*.'

'I told him it was unworthy of him to abuse a gallant, a magnificent profession. I told him there's no type so fine as that of the soldier doing his duty.'

'That's essentially *your* type, my dear boy.' Young Lechmere blushed; he couldn't make out – and the danger was naturally unexpected to him – whether at that moment he didn't exist mainly for the recreation of his friend. But he was partly reassured by the genial way this friend continued, laying a hand on his shoulder: 'Keep *at* him that way! We may do something. I'm in any case extremely obliged to you.'

Another doubt however remained unassuaged – a doubt which led him to overflow yet again before they dropped the painful subject: 'He *doesn't* care! But it's awfully odd he shouldn't!'

'So it is, but remember what you said this afternoon – I mean about your not advising people to make insinuations to *you*.'

'I believe I should knock the beggar down!' said young Lechmere. Mr Coyle had got up; the conversation had taken place while they sat together after Mrs Coyle's withdrawal from the dinner table, and the head of the establishment administered to his candid charge, on principles that were a part of his thoroughness, a glass of excellent claret. The disciple in question, also on his feet, lingered an instant, not for another 'go', as he would have called it, at the decanter, but to wipe his microscopic moustache with prolonged and unusual care. His companion saw he had something to bring out which required a final effort, and waited for him an instant with a hand on the knob of the door. Then as young Lechmere drew nearer Spencer Coyle grew conscious of an unwonted intensity in the round and ingenuous face. The boy was nervous, but tried to behave like a man of the world. 'Of course it's between ourselves,' he stammered, 'and I wouldn't breathe such a word to anyone who wasn't interested in poor Wingrave as you are. But do you think he funks it?'

Mr Coyle looked at him so hard an instant that he was visibly frightened at what he had said. 'Funks it! Funks what?'

'Why what we're talking about – the service.' Young Lechmere gave a little gulp and added with a want of active wit almost pathetic to Spencer Coyle: 'The dangers, you know!'

'Do you mean he's thinking of his skin?'

Young Lechmere's eyes expanded appealingly, and what his instructor saw in his pink face – even thinking he saw a tear – was the dread of a disappointment shocking in the degree in which the loyalty of admiration had been great.

'Is he – is he beastly *afraid*?' repeated the honest lad with a quaver of suspense.

'Dear no!' said Spencer Coyle, turning his back.

On which young Lechmere felt a little snubbed and even a little ashamed. But still more he felt relieved.

CHAPTER 3

Less than a week after this, the elder man received a note from Miss Wingrave, who had immediately quitted London with her nephew. She proposed he should come down to Paramore for the following Sunday – Owen was really so tiresome. On the spot, in that house of examples and memories and in combination with her poor dear father, who was 'dreadfully annoyed', it might be worth their while to make a last stand. Mr Coyle read between the lines of this letter that the party at Paramore had got over a good deal of ground since Miss Wingrave, in Baker Street, had treated his despair as superficial. She wasn't an insinuating woman, but she went so far as to put the question on the ground of his conferring a particular favour on an afflicted family; and she expressed the pleasure it would give them should he be accompanied by Mrs Coyle, for whom she enclosed a separate invitation. She mentioned that she was also writing, subject to Mr Coyle's approval, to young Lechmere. She thought such a nice manly boy might do her wretched nephew some good. The celebrated crammer decided to embrace this occasion; and now it was the case not so much that he was angry as that he was anxious. As he directed his answer to Miss Wingrave's letter, he caught himself smiling at the thought that at bottom he was going to defend his ex-pupil rather than to give him away. He said to his wife, who was a fair fresh slow woman – a person of much more presence than himself – that she had better take Miss Wingrave at her word: it was such an extraordinary, such a fascinating specimen of an old English home. This last allusion was softly sarcastic – he had accused the good lady more than once of being in love with Owen Wingrave. She admitted that she was, she even gloried in her passion; which shows that the subject, between them, was treated in a liberal spirit. She carried out the joke by accepting the invitation with eagerness. Young Lechmere was delighted to do the same; his instructor had good-naturedly taken the view that the little break would freshen him up for his last spurt.

It was the fact that the occupants of Paramore did indeed take their trouble hard that struck our friend after he had been an hour or two in that fine old house. This very short second visit, beginning on the Saturday evening, was to constitute the strangest episode of his life. As soon as he found himself in private with his wife – they had retired to dress for dinner – they called each other's attention with effusion and almost with alarm to the sinister gloom diffused through the place. The house was admirable from its old grey front, which came forward in wings so as to form three sides of a square, but Mrs Coyle made no scruple to declare that if she had known in advance the sort of impression she was going to receive she would never have put her foot in it. She characterised it as 'uncanny' and as looking wicked and weird, and she accused her husband of not having warned her properly. He had named to her in advance some of the appearances she was to expect, but while she almost feverishly dressed she had innumerable questions to ask. He hadn't told her about the girl, the extraordinary girl, Miss Julian – that is, he hadn't told her that this young lady, who in plain terms was a mere dependant, would be in effect, and as a consequence of the way she carried herself, the most important person in the house. Mrs Coyle was already prepared to announce that she hated Miss Julian's affectations. Her husband above all hadn't told her that they should find their young charge looking five years older.

'I couldn't imagine that,' Spencer said, 'nor that the character of the crisis here would be quite so perceptible. But I suggested to Miss Wingrave the other day that they should press her nephew in real earnest, and she has taken me at my word. They've cut off his supplies – they're trying to starve him out. That's not what I meant – but indeed I don't quite *know* today what I meant. Owen feels the pressure, but he won't yield.' The strange thing was that, now he was there, the brooding little coach knew still better, even while half-closing his eyes to it, that his own spirit had been caught up by a wave of reaction. If he was there it was because he was on poor Owen's side. His whole impression, his whole apprehension, had on the spot become much deeper. There was something in the young fanatic's very resistance that began to charm him. When his wife, in the intimacy of the conference I have mentioned, threw off the mask and commended even with extravagance the stand his pupil had taken (he was too good to be a horrid soldier and it was noble of him to suffer for his convictions – wasn't he as upright as a young hero, even though as pale as a Christian martyr?), the good lady only expressed the sympathy which, under cover of regarding his late inmate as a rare exception, he had already recognised in his own soul.

For, half an hour ago, after they had had superficial tea in the brown old hall of the house, that searcher into the reasons of things had proposed to him, before going to dress, a short turn outside, and had even, on the terrace, as they walked together to one of the far ends, passed his hand entreatingly into his companion's arm, permitting himself thus a familiarity unusual between pupil and master and calculated to show he had guessed whom he could most depend on to be kind to him. Spencer Coyle had on his own side guessed something, so that he wasn't surprised at the boy's having a particular confidence to make. He had felt on arriving that each member of the party would want to get hold of him first, and he knew that at that moment Jane Wingrave was peering through the ancient blur of one of the windows – the house had been modernised so little that the thick dim panes were three centuries old – to see whether her nephew looked as if he were poisoning the visitor's mind. Mr Coyle lost no time therefore in reminding the youth – though careful to turn it to a laugh as he did so – that he hadn't come down to Paramore to be corrupted. He had come down to make, face to face, a last appeal, which he hoped wouldn't be utterly vain. Owen smiled sadly as they went, asking him if he thought he had the general air of a fellow who was going to knock under.

'I think you look odd – I think you look ill,' Spencer Coyle said very honestly. They had paused at the end of the terrace.

'I've had to exercise a great power of resistance, and it rather takes it out of one.'

'Ah my dear boy, I wish your great power – for you evidently possess it – were exerted in a better cause!'

Owen Wingrave smiled down at his small but erect instructor. 'I don't believe that!' Then he added, to explain why: 'Isn't what you want (if you're so good as to think well of my character) to see me exert *most* power, in whatever direction? Well, this is the way I exert most.' He allowed he had had some terrible hours with his grandfather, who had denounced him in a way to make his hair stand up on his head. He had expected them not to like it, not a bit, but had had no idea they would make such a row. His aunt was different, but she was equally insulting. Oh they had made him feel they were ashamed of him; they accused him of putting a public dishonour on their name. He was the only one who had ever backed out – he was the first for three hundred years. Everyone had known he was to go up, and now everyone would know him for a young hypocrite who suddenly pretended to have scruples. They talked of his scruples as you wouldn't talk of a cannibal's god. His grandfather had called him outrageous names. 'He called me – he called me – ' Here Owen faltered and his voice failed him. He looked as haggard as was possible to a young man in such splendid health.

'I probably know!' said Spencer Coyle with a nervous laugh.

His companion's clouded eyes, as if following the last strange consequences of things, rested for an instant on a distant object. Then they met his own and for another moment sounded them deeply. 'It isn't true. No, it isn't. It's not *that*!'

'I don't suppose it is! But what *do* you propose instead of it?'

'Instead of what?'

'Instead of the stupid solution of war. If you take that away, you should suggest at least a substitute.'

'That's for the people in charge, for governments and cabinets,' said Owen. '*They'll* arrive soon enough at a substitute, in the particular case, if they're made to understand that they'll be hanged – and also drawn and quartered – if they don't find one. Make it a capital crime; *that* will quicken the wits of ministers!' His eyes brightened as he spoke, and he looked assured and exalted. Mr Coyle gave a sigh of sad surrender – it was really a stiff obsession. He saw the moment after this when Owen was on the point of asking if he too thought him a coward; but he was relieved to be able to judge that he either didn't suspect him of it or shrank uncomfortably from putting the question to the test. Spencer Coyle wished to show confidence, but somehow a direct assurance that he didn't doubt of his courage was too gross a compliment – it would be like saying he didn't doubt of his honesty. The difficulty was presently averted by Owen's continuing: 'My grandfather can't break the entail, but I shall have nothing but this place, which, as you know, is small and, with the way rents are going, has quite ceased to yield an income. He has some money – not much, but such as it is he cuts me off. My aunt does the same – she has let me know her intentions. She was to have left me her six hundred a year. It was all settled, but now what's definite is that I don't get a penny of it if I give up the army. I must add in fairness that I have from my mother three hundred a year of my own. And I tell you the simple truth when I say I don't care a rap for the loss of the money.' The young man drew the long slow breath of a creature in pain; then he added: '*That's* not what worries me!'

'What are you going to do instead then?' his friend asked without other comment.

'I don't know – perhaps nothing. Nothing great at all events. Only something peaceful!'

Owen gave a weary smile, as if, worried as he was, he could yet appreciate the humorous effect of such a declaration from a Wingrave; but what it suggested to his guest, who looked up at him with a sense that he was after all not a Wingrave for nothing and had a military steadiness under fire, was the exasperation that such a profession, made in such a way and striking them as the last word of the inglorious, might well have produced on the part of his grandfather and his aunt. 'Perhaps nothing' – when he might carry on the great tradition! Yes, he wasn't weak, and he was interesting; but there was clearly a point of view from which he was provoking. 'What *is* it then that worries you?' Mr Coyle demanded.

'Oh the house – the very air and feeling of it. There are strange voices in it that seem to mutter at me – to say dreadful things as I pass. I mean the general consciousness and responsibility of what I'm doing. Of course it hasn't been easy for me – anything rather! I assure you I don't enjoy it.' With a light in them that was like a longing for justice, Owen again bent his eyes on those of the little coach; then he pursued: 'I've started up all the old ghosts. The very portraits glower at me on the walls. There's one of my great-great-grandfather (the one the extraordinary story you know is about – the old fellow who hangs on the second landing of the big staircase) that fairly stirs on the canvas, just heaves a little, when I come near it. I have to go up and down stairs – it's rather awkward! It's what my aunt calls the family circle, and they sit, ever so grimly, in judgement. The circle's all constituted here, it's a kind of awful encompassing presence, it stretches away into the past, and when I came back with her the other day Miss Wingrave told me I wouldn't have the impudence to stand in the midst of it and say such things. I *had* to say them to my grandfather; but now that I've said them it seems to me the question's ended. I want to go away – I don't care if I never come back again.'

'Oh you *are* a soldier; you must fight it out!' Mr Coyle laughed.

The young man seemed discouraged at his levity, but as they turned round, strolling back in the direction from which they had come, he himself smiled faintly after an instant and replied: 'Ah we're tainted – all!'

They walked in silence part of the way to the old portico; then the elder of the pair, stopping short after having assured himself he was at a sufficient distance from the house not to be heard, suddenly put the question: 'What does Miss Julian say?'

'Miss Julian?' Owen had perceptibly coloured.

'I'm sure *she* hasn't concealed her opinion.'

'Oh it's the opinion of the family circle, for she's a member of it of course. And then she has her own as well.'

'Her own opinion?'

'Her own family circle.'

'Do you mean her mother – that patient lady?'

'I mean more particularly her father, who fell in battle. And her grandfather, and *his* father, and her uncles and great-uncles – they all fell in battle.'

Mr Coyle, his face now rather oddly set, took it in.

'Hasn't the sacrifice of so many lives been sufficient? Why should she sacrifice *you*?'

'Oh she *hates* me!' Owen declared as they resumed their walk.

'Ah the hatred of pretty girls for fine young men!' cried Spencer Coyle.

He didn't believe in it, but his wife did, it appeared perfectly, when he mentioned this conversation while, in the fashion that has been described, the visitors dressed for dinner. Mrs Coyle had already discovered that nothing could have been nastier than Miss Julian's manner to the disgraced youth during the half-hour the party had spent in the hall; and it was this lady's judgement that one must have had no eyes in one's head not to see that she was already trying outrageously to flirt with young Lechmere. It was a pity they had brought that silly boy: he was down in the hall with the creature at that moment. Spencer Coyle's version was different – he believed finer elements involved. The girl's footing in the house was inexplicable on any ground save that of her being predestined to Miss Wingrave's nephew. As the niece of Miss Wingrave's own unhappy intended, she had been devoted early by this lady to the office of healing by a union with the hope of the race the tragic breach that had separated their elders; and if in reply to this it was to be said that a girl of spirit couldn't enjoy in such a matter having her duty cut out for her, Owen's enlightened friend was ready with the argument that a young person in Miss Julian's position would never be such a fool as really to quarrel with a capital chance. She was familiar at Paramore and she felt safe; therefore she might treat herself to the amusement of pretending she had her option. It was all innocent tricks and airs. She had a curious charm, and it was vain to pretend that the heir of that house wouldn't seem good enough to a girl, clever as she might be, of eighteen. Mrs Coyle reminded her husband that their late charge was precisely now *not* of that house: this question was among the articles that exercised their wits after the two men had taken the turn on the terrace. Spencer then mentioned to his wife that Owen was afraid of the portrait of his great-great-grandfather. He would show it to her, since she hadn't noticed it, on their way downstairs.

'Why of his great-great-grandfather more than of any of the others?'

'Oh because he's the most formidable. He's the one who's sometimes seen.'

'Seen where?' Mrs Coyle had turned round with a jerk.

'In the room he was found dead in – the White Room they've always called it.'

'Do you mean to say the house has a proved *ghost*?' Mrs Coyle almost shrieked. 'You brought me here without telling me?'

'Didn't I mention it after my other visit?'

'Not a word. You only talked about Miss Wingrave.'

'Oh I was full of the story – you've simply forgotten.'

'Then you should have reminded me!'

'If I had thought of it, I'd have held my peace – for you wouldn't have come.'

'I wish indeed I hadn't!' cried Mrs Coyle. 'But what,' she immediately asked, '*is* the story?'

'Oh a deed of violence that took place here ages ago. I think it was in George the Second's time that Colonel Wingrave, one of their ancestors, struck in a fit of passion one of his children, a lad just growing up, a blow on the head of which the unhappy child died. The matter was hushed up for the hour and some other explanation put about. The poor boy was laid out in one of those rooms on the other side of the house, and amid strange smothered rumours the funeral was hurried on. The next morning, when the household assembled, Colonel Wingrave was missing; he was looked for vainly, and at last it occurred to someone that he might perhaps be in the room from which his child had been carried to burial. The seeker knocked without an answer – then opened the door. The poor man lay dead on the floor, in his clothes, as if he had reeled and fallen back, without a wound, without a mark, without anything in his appearance to indicate that he had either struggled or suffered. He was a strong sound man – there was nothing to account for such a stroke. He's supposed to have gone to the room during the night, just before going to bed, in some fit of compunction or some fascination of dread. It was only after this that the truth about the boy came out. But no one ever sleeps in the room.'

Mrs Coyle had fairly turned pale. 'I hope not indeed! Thank heaven they haven't put *us* there!'

'We're at a comfortable distance – I know the scene of the event.'

'Do you mean you've been in – ?'

'For a few moments. They're rather proud of the place and my young friend showed it me when I was here before.'

Mrs Coyle stared. 'And what is it like?'

'Simply an empty dull old-fashioned bedroom, rather big and furnished with the things of the "period". It's panelled from floor to ceiling, and the panels evidently, years and years ago, were painted white. But the paint has darkened with time and there are three or four quaint little ancient "samplers", framed and glazed, hung on the walls.'

Mrs Coyle looked round with a shudder. 'I'm glad there are no samplers here! I never heard anything so jumpy! Come down to dinner.'

On the staircase as they went her husband showed her the portrait of Colonel Wingrave – a representation, with some force and style, for the place and period, of a gentleman with a hard handsome face, in a red coat and a peruke. Mrs Coyle pronounced his descendant old Sir Philip wonderfully like him; and her husband could fancy, though he kept it to himself, that if one should have the courage to walk the old corridors of Paramore at night, one might meet a figure that resembled him roaming, with the restlessness of a ghost, hand in hand with the figure of a tall boy. As he proceeded to the drawing-room with his wife he found himself suddenly wishing he had made more of a point of his pupil's going to Eastbourne. The evening how-ever seemed to have taken upon itself to dissipate any such whimsical forebodings, for the grimness of the family circle, as he had preconceived its composition, was mitigated by an infusion of the 'neighbourhood'. The company at dinner was recruited by two cheerful couples, one of them the vicar and his wife, and by a silent young man who had come down to fish. This was a relief to Mr Coyle, who had begun to wonder what was after all expected of him and why he had been such a fool as to come, and who now felt that for the first hours at least the situation wouldn't have directly to be dealt with. Indeed he found, as he had found before, sufficient occupation for his ingenuity in reading the various symptoms of which the social scene that spread about him was an expression. He should probably have a trying day on the morrow: he foresaw the difficulty of the long decorous Sunday and how dry Jane Wingrave's ideas, elicited in strenuous conference, would taste. She and her father would make him feel they depended upon him for the impossible, and if they should try to associate him with too tactless a policy he might end by telling them what he thought of it – an accident not required to make his visit a depressed mistake. The old man's actual design was evidently to let their friends see in it a positive mark of their being all right. The presence of the great London coach was tantamount to a profession of faith in the results of the impending examination. It had clearly been obtained from Owen, rather to the principal visitor's surprise, that he would do nothing to interfere with the apparent concord. He let the allusions to his hard work pass and, holding his tongue about his affairs, talked to the ladies as amicably as if he hadn't been 'cut off'. When Mr Coyle looked at him once or twice across the table, catching his eye, which showed an indefinable passion, he found a puzzling pathos in his laughing face: one couldn't resist a pang for a young lamb so visibly marked for sacrifice. 'Hang him, what a pity he's such a fighter!' he privately sighed – and with a want of logic that was only superficial.

This idea however would have absorbed him more if so much of his attention hadn't been for Kate Julian, who now that he had her well before him struck him as a remarkable and even as a possibly interesting young woman. The interest resided not in any extra-ordinary prettiness, for if she was handsome, with her long Eastern eyes, her magnificent hair and her general unabashed originality, he had seen complexions rosier and features that pleased him more: it dwelt in a strange impression that she gave of being exactly the sort of person whom, in her position, common considerations, those of prudence and perhaps even a little decorum, would have enjoined on her not to be. She was what was vulgarly termed a dependant – penniless, patronised, tolerated; but something in all her air conveyed that if her situation was inferior her spirit, to make up for it, was above precautions or submissions. It wasn't in the least that she was aggressive – she was too indifferent for that; it was only as if, having nothing either to gain or to lose, she could afford to do as she liked. It occurred to Spencer Coyle that she might really have had more at stake than her imagination appeared to take account of; whatever this quantity might be, at any rate, he had never seen a young woman at less pains to keep the safe side. He wondered inevitably what terms prevailed between Jane Wingrave and such an inmate as this; but those questions of course were unfathomable deeps. Perhaps keen Kate lorded it even over her protectress. The other time he was at Paramore he had received an impression that, with Sir Philip beside her, the girl could fight with her back to the wall. She amused Sir Philip, she charmed him, and he liked people who weren't afraid; between him and his daughter moreover there was no doubt which was the higher in command. Miss Wingrave took many things for granted, and most of all the rigour of discipline and the fate of the vanquished and the captive.

But between their clever boy and so original a companion of his childhood what odd relation would have grown up? It couldn't be indifference, and yet on the part of happy handsome youthful creatures it was still less likely to be aversion. They weren't Paul and Virginia, but they must have had their common summer and their idyll: no nice girl could have disliked such a nice fellow for anything but not liking *her*, and no nice fellow could have resisted such propinquity. Mr Coyle remembered indeed that Mrs Julian had spoken to him as if the propinquity had been by no means constant, owing to her daughter's absences at school, to say nothing of Owen's; her visits to a few friends who were so kind as to 'take' her from time to time; her sojourns in London – so difficult to manage, but still managed by God's help – for 'advantages', for drawing and singing, especially drawing, or rather painting in oils, for which she had gained high credit. But the good lady had also mentioned that the young people were quite brother and sister, which *was* a little, after all, like Paul and Virginia. Mrs Coyle had been right, and it was apparent that Virginia was doing her best to make the time pass agreeably for young Lechmere. There was no such whirl of conversation as to render it an effort for our critic to reflect on these things: the tone of the occasion, thanks principally to the other guests, was not disposed to stray – it tended to the repetition of anecdote and the discussion of rents, topics that huddled together like uneasy animals. He could judge how intensely his hosts wished the evening to pass off as if nothing had happened; and this gave him the measure of their private resentment. Before dinner was over he found himself fidgety about his second pupil. Young Lechmere, since he began to cram, had done all that might have been expected of him; but this couldn't blind his instructor to a present perception of his being in moments of relaxation as innocent as a babe. Mr Coyle had considered that the amusements of Paramore would probably give him a fillip, and the poor youth's manner testified to the soundness of the forecast. The fillip had been unmistakeably administered; it had come in the form of a revelation. The light on young Lechmere's brow announced with a candour that was almost an appeal for compassion, or at least a deprecation of ridicule, that he had never seen anything like Miss Julian.

CHAPTER 4

In the drawing-room after dinner, the girl found a chance to approach Owen's late preceptor. She stood before him a moment, smiling while she opened and shut her fan, and then said abruptly, raising her strange eyes: 'I know what you've come for, but it isn't any use.'

'I've come to look after *you* a little. Isn't *that* any use?'

'It's very kind. But I'm not the question of the hour. You won't do anything with Owen.'

Spencer Coyle hesitated a moment. 'What will *you* do with his young friend?'

She stared, looked round her. 'Mr Lechmere? Oh poor little lad! We've been talking about Owen. He admires him so.'

'So do I. I should tell you that.'

'So do we all. That's why we're in such despair.'

'Personally then you'd *like* him to be a soldier?' the visitor asked.

'I've quite set my heart on it. I adore the army and I'm awfully fond of my old playmate,' said Miss Julian.

Spencer recalled the young man's own different version of her attitude; but he judged it loyal not to challenge her. 'It's not conceivable that your old playmate shouldn't be fond of you. He must therefore wish to please you; and I don't see why – between you, such clever young people as you are! – you don't set the matter right.'

'Wish to please me!' Miss Julian echoed. 'I'm sorry to say he shows no such desire. He thinks me an impudent wretch. I've told him what I think of *him*, and he simply hates me.'

'But you think so highly! You just told me you admire him.'

'His talents, his possibilities, yes; even his personal appearance, if I may allude to such a matter. But I don't admire his present behaviour.'

'Have you had the question out with him?' Spencer asked.

'Oh yes, I've ventured to be frank – the occasion seemed to excuse it. He couldn't like what I said.'

'What did you say?'

The girl, thinking a moment, opened and shut her fan again. 'Why – as we're such good old friends – that such conduct doesn't begin to be that of a gentleman!'

After she had spoken her eyes met Mr Coyle's, who looked into their ambiguous depths. 'What then would you have said without that tie?'

'How odd for *you* to ask that – in such a way!' she returned with a laugh. 'I don't understand your position: I thought your line was to *make* soldiers!'

'You should take my little joke. But, as regards Owen Wingrave, there's no "making" needed,' he declared. 'To my sense' – and the little crammer paused as with a consciousness of responsibility for his paradox – 'to my sense he *is*, in a high sense of the term, a fighting man.'

'Ah let him prove it!' she cried with impatience and turning short off.

Spencer Coyle let her go; something in her tone annoyed and even not a little shocked him. There had evidently been a violent passage between these young persons, and the reflection that such a matter was after all none of his business but troubled him the more. It was indeed a military house, and she was at any rate a damsel who placed her ideal of manhood – damsels doubtless always had their ideals of manhood – in the type of the belted warrior. It was a taste like another; but even a quarter of an hour later, finding himself near young Lechmere, in whom this type was embodied, Spencer Coyle was still so ruffled that he addressed the innocent lad with a certain magisterial dryness. 'You're under no pressure to sit up late, you know. That's not what I brought you down for.' The dinner guests were taking leave and the bedroom candles twinkled in a monitory row. Young Lechmere however was too agreeably agitated to be accessible to a snub: he had a happy preoccupation which almost engendered a grin.

'I'm only too eager for bedtime. Do you know there's an awfully jolly room?'

Coyle debated a moment as to whether he should take the allusion – then spoke from his general tension. 'Surely they haven't put you there?'

'No indeed: no one has passed a night in it for ages.

But that's exactly what I want to do – it would be tremendous fun.'

'And have you been trying to get Miss Julian's leave?'

'Oh *she* can't give it she says. But she believes in it, and she maintains that no man has ever dared.'

'No man *shall* ever!' said Spencer with decision. 'A fellow in your critical position in particular must have a quiet night.'

Young Lechmere gave a disappointed but reasonable sigh. 'Oh all right. But mayn't I sit up for a little go at Wingrave? I haven't had any yet.'

Mr Coyle looked at his watch. 'You may smoke *one* cigarette.'

He felt a hand on his shoulder and turned round to see his wife tilting candle grease upon his coat. The ladies were going to bed and it was Sir Philip's inveterate hour; but Mrs Coyle confided to her husband that after the dreadful things he had told her she positively declined to be left alone, for no matter how short an interval, in any part of the house. He promised to follow her within three minutes, and after the orthodox handshakes the ladies rustled away. The forms were kept up at Paramore as bravely as if the old house had no present intensity of heart-ache. The only one of which Coyle noticed the drop was some salutation to himself from Kate Julian. She gave him neither a word nor a glance, but he saw her look hard at Owen. Her mother, timid and pitying, was apparently the only person from whom this young man caught an inclination of the head. Miss Wingrave marshalled the three ladies – her little procession of twinkling tapers – up the wide oaken stairs and past the watching portrait of her ill-fated ancestor. Sir Philip's servant appeared and offered his arm to the old man, who turned a perpendicular back on poor Owen when the boy made a vague movement to anticipate this office. Mr Coyle learned later that before Owen had forfeited favour it had always, when he was at home, been his privilege at bedtime to conduct his grandfather ceremoniously to rest. Sir Philip's habits were contemptuously different now. His apartments were on the lower floor and he shuffled stiffly off to them with his valet's help, after fixing for a moment significantly on the most responsible of his visitors the thick red ray, like the glow of stirred embers, that always made his eyes conflict oddly with his mild manners. They seemed to say to poor Spencer 'We'll let the young scoundrel have it tomorrow!' One might have gathered from them that the young scoundrel, who had now strolled to the other end of the hall, had at least forged a cheque. His friend watched him an instant, saw him drop nervously into a chair and then with a restless movement get up. The same movement brought him back to where Mr Coyle stood addressing a last injunction to young Lechmere.

'I'm going to bed and I should like you particularly to conform to what I said to you a short time ago. Smoke a single cigarette with our host here and then go to your room. You'll have me down on you if I hear of your having, during the night, tried any preposterous games.' Young Lechmere, looking down with his hands in his pockets, said nothing – he only poked at the corner of a rug with his toe; so that his fellow visitor, dissatisfied with so tacit a pledge, presently went on to Owen: 'I must request you, Wingrave, not to keep so sensitive a subject sitting up – and indeed to put him to bed and turn his key in the door.' As Owen stared an instant, apparently not understanding the motive of so much solicitude, he added: 'Lechmere has a morbid curiosity about one of your legends – of your historic rooms. Nip it in the bud.'

'Oh the legend's rather good, but I'm afraid the room's an awful sell!' Owen laughed.

'You know you don't *believe* that, my boy!' young Lechmere returned.

'I don't think he does' – Mr Coyle noticed Owen's mottled flush.

'He wouldn't try a night there himself!' their companion pursued.

'I know who told you that,' said Owen, lighting a cigarette in an embarrassed way at the candle, without offering one to either of his friends.

'Well, what if she did?' asked the younger of these gentlemen, rather red. 'Do you want them *all* yourself?' he continued facetiously, fumbling in the cigarette-box.

Owen Wingrave only smoked quietly; then he brought out: 'Yes – what if she did? But she doesn't know,' he added.

'She doesn't know what?'

'She doesn't know anything! – I'll tuck him in!'

Owen went on gaily to Mr Coyle, who saw that his presence, now a certain note had been struck, made the young men uncomfortable. He was curious, but there were discretions and delicacies, with his pupils, that he had always pretended to practise; scruples which however didn't prevent, as he took his way upstairs, his recommending them not to be donkeys.

At the top of the staircase, to his surprise, he met

Miss Julian, who was apparently going down again. She hadn't begun to undress, nor was she perceptibly disconcerted at seeing him. She nevertheless, in a manner slightly at variance with the rigour with which she had overlooked him ten minutes before, dropped the words: 'I'm going down to look for something. I've lost a jewel.'

'A jewel?'

'A rather good turquoise, out of my locket. As it's the only *real* ornament I've the honour to possess – !' And she began to descend.

'Shall I go with you and help you?' asked Spencer Coyle.

She paused a few steps below him, looking back with her Oriental eyes. 'Don't I hear our friends' voices in the hall?'

'Those remarkable young men are there.'

'*They'll* help me.' And Kate Julian passed down.

Spencer Coyle was tempted to follow her, but remembering his standard of tact, he rejoined his wife in their apartment. He delayed nevertheless to go to bed and, though he looked into his dressing-room, couldn't bring himself even to take off his coat. He pretended for half an hour to read a novel; after which, quietly, or perhaps I should say agitatedly, he stepped from the dressing-room into the corridor. He followed this passage to the door of the room he knew to have been assigned to young Lechmere and was comforted to see it closed. Half an hour earlier he had noticed it stand open; therefore he could take for granted the bewildered boy had come to bed. It was of this he had wished to assure himself, and having done so he was on the point of retreating. But at the same instant he heard a sound in the room – the occupant was doing, at the window, something that showed him he might knock without the reproach of waking his pupil up. Young Lechmere came in fact to the door in his shirt and trousers. He admitted his visitor in some surprise, and when the door was closed again the latter said: 'I don't want to make your life a burden, but I had it on my conscience to see for myself that you're not exposed to undue excitement.'

'Oh there's plenty of that!' said the ingenuous youth. 'Miss Julian came down again.'

'To look for a turquoise?'

'So she said.'

'Did she find it?'

'I don't know. I came up. I left her with poor Owen.'

'Quite the right thing,' said Spencer Coyle.

'I don't know,' young Lechmere repeated uneasily. 'I left them quarrelling.'

'What about?'

'I don't understand. They're a quaint pair!'

Spencer turned it over. He had, fundamentally, principles and high decencies, but what he had in particular just now was a curiosity, or rather, to recognise it for what it was, a sympathy, which brushed them away. 'Does it strike you that *she's* down on him?' he permitted himself to enquire.

'Rather! – when she tells him he lies!'

'What do you mean?'

'Why before *me*. It made me leave them; it was getting too hot. I stupidly brought up the question of that bad room again, and said how sorry I was I had had to promise you not to try my luck with it.'

'You can't pry about in that gross way in other people's houses – you can't take such liberties, you know!' Mr Coyle interjected.

'I'm all right – see how good I am. I don't want to go *near* the place!' said young Lechmere confidingly. 'Miss Julian said to me "Oh I dare say *you'd* risk it, but" – and she turned and laughed at poor Owen – "that's more than we can expect of a gentleman who has taken *his* extraordinary line." I could see that something had already passed between them on the subject – some teasing or challenging of hers. It may have been only chaff, but his chucking the profession had evidently brought up the question of the white feather – I mean of his pluck.'

'And what did Owen say?'

'Nothing at first; but presently he brought out very quietly: "I spent all last night in the confounded place." We both stared and cried out at this and I asked him what he had seen there. He said he had seen nothing, and Miss Julian replied that he ought to tell his story better than that – he ought to make something good of it. "It's not a story – it's a simple fact," said he; on which she jeered at him and wanted to know why, if he had done it, he hadn't told her in the morning, since he knew what she thought of him. "I know, my dear, but I don't care," the poor devil said. This made her angry, and she asked him quite seriously whether he'd care if he should know she believed him to be trying to deceive us.'

'Ah what a brute!' cried Spencer Coyle.

'She's a most extraordinary girl – I don't know what she's up to,' young Lechmere quite panted.

'Extraordinary indeed – to be romping and bandying words at that hour of the night with fast young men!'

But young Lechmere made his distinction. 'I mean because I think she likes him.'

Mr Coyle was so struck with this unwonted symptom of subtlety that he flashed out: 'And do you think he likes *her*?'

It produced on his pupil's part a drop and a plaintive sigh. 'I don't know – I give it up! – But I'm sure he *did* see something or hear something,' the youth added.

'In that ridiculous place? What makes you sure?'

'Well, because he looks as if he had. I've an idea you can tell – in such a case. He behaves as if he had.'

'Why then shouldn't he name it?'

Young Lechmere wondered and found. 'Perhaps it's too bad to mention.'

Spencer Coyle gave a laugh. 'Aren't you glad then *you're* not in it?'

'Uncommonly!'

'Go to bed, you goose,' Spencer said with renewed nervous derision. 'But before you go, tell me how he met her charge that he was trying to deceive you.'

' "Take me there yourself then and lock me in!" '

'And *did* she take him?'

'I don't know – I came up.'

He exchanged a long look with his pupil. 'I don't think they're in the hall now. Where's Owen's own room?'

'I haven't the least idea.'

Mr Coyle was at a loss; he was in equal ignorance and he couldn't go about trying doors. He bade young Lechmere sink to slumber; after which he came out into the passage. He asked himself if he should be able to find his way to the room Owen had formerly shown him, remembering that in common with many of the others it had its ancient name painted on it. But the corridors of Paramore were intricate; moreover some of the servants would still be up, and he didn't wish to appear unduly to prowl. He went back to his own quarters, where Mrs Coyle soon noted the continuance of his inability to rest. As she confessed for her own part, in the dreadful place, to an increased sense of 'creepiness', they spent the early part of the night in conversation, so that a portion of their vigil was inevitably beguiled by her husband's account of his colloquy with little Lechmere and by their exchange of opinions upon it. Towards two o'clock, Mrs Coyle became so nervous about their persecuted young friend, and so possessed by the fear that that wicked girl had availed herself of his invitation to put him to an abominable test, that she begged her husband to go and look into the matter at whatever cost to his own tranquillity. But Spencer, perversely, had ended, as the perfect stillness of the night settled upon them, by charming himself into a pale acceptance of Owen's readiness to face God knew what unholy strain – an exposure the more trying to excited sensibilities as the poor boy had now learned by the ordeal of the previous night how resolute an effort he should have to make. 'I hope he *is* there,' he said to his wife: 'it puts them all so hideously in the wrong!' At any rate, he couldn't take on himself to explore a house he knew so little. He was inconsequent – he didn't prepare for bed. He sat in the dressing-room with his light and his novel – he waited to find himself nod. At last however Mrs Coyle turned over and ceased to talk, and at last too he fell asleep in his chair. How long he slept he knew afterwards only by computation; what he knew to begin with was that he had started up in confusion and under the shock of an appalling sound. His consciousness cleared itself fast, helped doubtless by a confirmatory cry of horror from his wife's room. But he gave no heed to his wife; he had already bounded into the passage. There the sound was repeated – it was the 'Help! help!' of a woman in agonised terror. It came from a distant quarter of the house, but the quarter was sufficiently indicated. He rushed straight before him, the sound of opening doors and alarmed voices in his ears and the faintness of the early dawn in his eyes. At a turn of one of the passages, he came upon the white figure of a girl in a swoon on a bench, and in the vividness of the revelation he read as he went that Kate Julian, stricken in her pride too late with a chill of compunction for what she had mockingly done, had, after coming to release the victim of her derision, reeled away, overwhelmed, from the catastrophe that was her work – the catastrophe that the next moment he found himself aghast at on the threshold of an open door. Owen Wingrave, dressed as he had last seen him, lay dead on the spot on which his ancestor had been found. He was all the young soldier on the gained field.

AFTERWORD

To bring the bad dead back to life for a second round of badness is to warrant them as indeed prodigious, and to become hence as shy of specifications as of a waiting anti-climax.

HENRY JAMES
Preface to Volume XII
of the New York Edition of
The Novels and Tales of Henry James (1908)

It was perhaps inevitable that Henry James (1843–1916) should turn his hand to writing tales of the supernatural, examining the psychological and emotional effects of hauntings, for his father, Henry James senior, a writer on religious and social issues, experienced a terrifying paranormal incident and underwent a religious conversion to Spiritualism. Apparently one evening he was overtaken with powerful feelings of terror as he sensed 'a damned shape' squatting invisibly in the corner of the room where he was sitting. Also, the author's brother, William James, a distinguished philosopher and psychologist, founded the American Society of Psychical Research which investigated ghostly and other paranormal phenomena. With such strong familial influences, it is no wonder that Henry James brought these subjects into his fiction, which he did from his early days. His first attempts in the genre were penned when he was twenty-five. In 1868 James published two short stories with supernatural themes: 'A Romance of Certain Old Clothes' and 'De Gray: A Romance'. The fact that the word 'romance' features in both titles suggests perhaps that at this juncture James was unsure as to what extent the supernatural elements in the stories were to be capable of explanation. By comparison with his later works these stories are weak and simplistic. A more successful tale, 'The Ghostly Rental', written eight years later in 1876, reveals greater assurance and indicates maturity of thought in both complexity and style. A house is haunted, supposedly by the ghost of a daughter who has died as a result of her father's cruelty. However, the girl is not dead but is taking a cruel revenge on her unwitting father. His health suffers through remorse and he dies. It is then that the girl is haunted – by the ghost of her father.

When James came to write his supernatural masterpiece, *The Turn of the Screw*, in 1898, he had achieved great success as a mainstream novelist with works such as *Portrait of a Lady*, *The Bostonians* and *Washington Square*. These novels were in essence narrative romances with highly developed characters set against a background of illuminating social commentary on politics, class and status, as well as explorations of the themes of personal freedom, feminism and morality. He employed the technique of interior monologue: this method of writing from the point of view of a character within a tale allowed James to explore issues relating to the consciousness and perceptions of the narrator. It was the use of this approach in *The Turn of the Screw* which helped to create its dark compelling power over the reader.

The story begins in a rather traditional way: ghost

stories are being told after dinner in a large house on Christmas Eve and one of the party claims that his exceeds all the others because it is true and 'dreadful'. While this introduction to the story proper may well seem somewhat clichéd, James manages in the Prologue not only to set up the situation in which the narrative takes place but, more importantly, he also gives the reader a character assessment of the female narrator whose observations and sensibilities will be the driving force of the story. We learn that at the time the incidents took place she was 'young, untried, nervous', but also that she was 'charming' 'agreeable' and 'worthy'; in other words we are meant to like her and trust her. These are important details if we are to believe all she recounts in her strange story.

Nevertheless, in its bare outline, the narrative has a fairly conventional structure and James's notations in his journals reveal that the basic plot tends to follow the path of the traditional ghost story. Indeed, he referred to the tale as 'this perfectly independent and irresponsible little fiction'. However, his tight control of the narrative and the psychological spice which he adds to the simple outline darken and cloud the issues, adding richness and juicy uncertainties which he refrains from resolving. In his dismissal of the story as an 'irresponsible little fiction' we fear James does protest too much. At the time he composed the novella he was becoming more and more 'shy of specifications', of spelling out motives and purposes. He knew that human beings do not function on such a practical and literal level. Allowances must be made for unpredictable and irrational actions. All his fiction was conceived in such a way that subtle and elusive feelings and relationships were presented in a realistic fashion. Also, one also must not forget that the imagination guides the writer's hand and does not always explain its secrets.

One of the key areas of discussion regarding this story concerns the governess's perceptions: are the ghosts real or are they just figments of her disturbed imagination? The fact that this question is asked at all demonstrates the unsettling nature of the story. Initially there were no doubts in the minds of those who reviewed the novella on its original publication as to whether this was a ghost story or the recollections of a disturbed young woman. It was simply regarded as the tale of an heroic governess struggling against supernatural forces of evil which threaten to corrupt and destroy two young children. However later critics have looked beyond the surface telling of the tale to discover murky psychological elements within the text. In 1934, the influential critic Edmund Wilson wrote an article in the literary magazine *Hound and Horn*, 'The Ambiguities of Henry James', in which he probed the possible double meanings in the story. In essence he maintained that the governess was suffering from neurotic 'sex repression', that she was in love with the children's guardian – a fact established in the Preface – and that Quint and Jessel were the projection of her own sexual desires or fears. Her instant passion for the children's guardian, whom she only met on two occasions, certainly suggests not only that the governess was an impressionable young woman but that she harboured deep sexual feelings which were eager to be released. However, whatever emotional undercurrents were swirling through the governess's psyche, surely she could not have described Quint with such accuracy without actually seeing an apparition? This dilemma has prompted much critical debate over the years and more modern readers of the story seem to think that the truth of the matter – if such a thing can be considered in a work of fiction – is that the governess's repressed sexuality made her all the more vulnerable to the evil interventions of the ghosts. Her heightened suscep-tibility explains why she saw the ghosts while the rest of the household were ignorant of their presence and influence.

Another area where James departs from the general format of the traditional ghost story is the way in which the governess becomes a crusader in the fight against evil. She is not merely a spectator but is determined to save the children from the demonic influence of the spectral Quint and Jessel. She believes that the ghosts are pursuing their nefarious intercourse with the children in order to take possession of their souls and corrupt them radically. The governess conceives that her mission is to save the children from this terrible fate by engaging in a ferocious moral struggle against these powerful malevolent forces from beyond the grave. Her strong belief is that she can exorcise the children if she is able catch them in the act of communing with the spirits and thereby force them to admit their unholy relationship and their infernal complicity with the ghosts. To her, this act will cleanse and save the children. Unfortunately, the governess is mis-guided in this belief and the results of this heroic metaphysical struggle are disastrous. Flora, the little girl, caught by the governess in the presence of the phantom Miss Jessel, is so tightly enmeshed in the ghost's power that she denies seeing the vision. Flora now holds the governess in abhorrence and regards her with such animosity that it seems best she is taken away from her circle of influence and protection. Similarly Miles is also pressured by the governess to acknowledge his relationship with Quint and his ghostly presence by pronouncing the man's name. In doing so, Miles dies in her arms. There is more ambiguity with his death for as he expires he cries, 'You devil.' To whom is he addressing this remark – the apparition of Quint or the governess herself? James leaves it to the reader to decide. However, the message of the novel seems clear: we cannot hope to defeat those evil spirits that come back from the grave to cause havoc. That is one of the most frightening aspects of this story.

The use of children in this scenario was also seen as daring at the time and added an extra frisson to the drama. A single child as victim would be chilling, but as one of the observers in the Prologue remarks:

> 'If the child gives the effect another turn of the screw, what do you say to *two* children – ?'
>
> 'We say, of course,' somebody exclaimed, 'that two children give two turns!'   [p. 9–10]

This notion is emphasised by the title. Of course, as already stated, what makes this tale darker and much more than a ghost story is the suggestion that these spirits are not there merely to frighten or to punish, as is often the case in ghost stories, but their purpose it seems is to corrupt two young children. In 1961, when the novella came to be made into a film (starring Deborah Kerr as the governess and with Jack Clayton directing), it was called *The Innocents*, emphasising the children's vulnerability and by implication the horror of what happens to them. No wonder the reviewer of the book in the New York weekly magazine, the *Independent* (5 January 1899), described the story as, 'the most hopelessly evil story that we have ever read in any literature'.

The darkness of the plot appealed to Benjamin Britten who wrote an opera based on James's novella. Britten seemed to have a penchant for stories concerning persecuted youth. One of his other major works was *Billy Budd* (1951), concerning the ill-treatment and hanging of an innocent young sailor who suffered from a stutter. *The Turn of the Screw* was first produced in 1954 with a libretto by Myfanwy Piper. The opera follows the plot of the novella closely but goes further in that it presents the ghosts of Quint and Miss Jessel in conversation. In Act 2, for example, they argue about who harmed whom first when they were alive, and accuse one another of not acting quickly enough to possess the children. Thematically, the libretto gives a central role to a line borrowed from William Butler Yeats's poem, 'The Second Coming': 'The ceremony of innocence is drowned.'

Putting aside for one moment whether one agrees with Wilson's Freudian theory that the ghosts are merely a projection of the governess's repressed sexual passions or whether one takes the view that the governess and her charges are in the presence of evil returned from the dead, it is appropriate to note that the real power of the story is in its telling. The subtle, mannered prose with its insidious and mounting use of terror and suspense are masterful. Henry James was at the peak of his powers, crafting from a comparatively simple plot a chilling masterpiece.

The success of the *The Turn of the Screw* and the critical attention it garnered seem to have surprised the author. Ten years after the original publication, he referred to the story as 'a piece of ingenuity pure and simple, of cold artistic calculation, an *amusette* to catch those who are not easily caught'. Still he would not be the first writer to underestimate the true greatness of his work.

While 'Owen Wingrave' is a lesser tale, it is not without its own power and fascination. It was first published in the Christmas number of the *Graphic* in 1892. In essence, the supernatural elements in the story are minimal. If anything they are used as a *deus ex machina* to prove the moral of the story, that war is not the only agency for the display of personal courage. It is interesting to note how the idea for the story developed by examining what James wrote in his personal notebook at the time:

> *March 26th, 1892*
> The idea of the *soldier* – produced a little by the fascinated perusal of Marbot's magnificent memoirs. The image, the type, the vision, the character, as a transmitted, hereditary, mystical, almost supernatural force, challenge, incentive, almost haunting, apparitional presence, in the life and consciousness of a descendant – a descendant of totally different temperament and range of qualities, yet subjected to a superstitious awe in relation to carrying out the tradition of absolutely *military* valour – personal bravery and honour. Sense of the difficulty – the impossibility, etc.;

sense of the ugliness, the blood, the carnage, the suffering. All the things make him dodge it – not from cowardice, but from suffering. Get *something* it is enjoined upon him to do – etc. I can't complete this indication now; but I will take it up again, as I see in it the glimmer of an idea for a small subject, though only dimly and confusedly – the subject, or rather the idea, of a brave soldierly act – an act of heroism – done in the very effort to evade all the ugly and brutal part of the religion, the sacrifice, and winning (in a tragic death?) the reward of gallantry – winning it from the apparitional ancestor. This is very crude and rough, but there is probably something in it which I shall extract.

May 8th, 1892, 34 De Vere Gardens
Can't I hammer out a little the idea – for a short tale – of the young soldier? – the young fellow who, though predestined, by every tradition of his race, to the profession of arms, has an insurmountable hatred of it – of the *bloody* side of it, the suffering, the ugliness, the cruelty; so that he determines to reject it for himself – to break with it and cast it off, and this in the face of every sort of coercion of opinion (on the part of others), of such pressure not to let the family honour, etc. (always gloriously connected with the army), break down, that there is a kind of degradation, an exposure to ridicule and ignominy in his apostasy. The idea should be that he fights, after all, exposes himself to possibilities of danger and death for his own view – acts the soldier, *is* the soldier, and of indefeasible soldierly race – proves to have been so – even in

this very effort of abjuration. The thing is to invent
the particular heroic situation in which he may have
found himself – show just *how* he has been a hero
even while throwing away his arms. It is a question
of a little subject for the *Graphic* – so I mustn't
make it 'psychological' – they understand that
no more than a donkey understands a violin. The
particular form of opposition, of coercion, that he
has to face, and the way his 'heroism' is *constatée*. It
must, for prettiness's sake, be *constatée* in the eyes
of some woman, some girl, whom he loves but
who has taken the line of despising him for his
renunciation – some *fille de soldat*, who is very
montée about the whole thing, very hard on him,
etc. But what the subject wants is to be distanced,
relegated into some picturesque little past when
the army occupied more place in life – poetised by
some slightly romantic setting. Even if one could
introduce a supernatural element in it – make it, I
mean, a little ghost-story; place it, the scene,
in some old country-house, in England at the
beginning of the present century – the time of the
Napoleonic Wars. It seems to me one might make
some *haunting* business that would give it a colour
without being ridiculous, and get in that way the
sort of pressure to which the young man is subjected.
I see it – it comes to me a little. He must die, of
course, be slain, as it were on his own battlefield,
the night spent in the haunted room in which the
ghost of some grim grandfather – some bloody
warrior of the race – or some father slain in the
Peninsular or at Waterloo – is supposed to make
himself visible.

These notes make it clear that unlike *The Turn of the Screw*, this story shuns any ambiguity of purpose and is quite clear in its precepts. It is an anti-war tale – the clue is in the title – where the supernatural elements are cleverly used in a unique fashion to bring James's point home firmly and clearly.

This story also received the attention of Benjamin Britten. He became familiar with it while working on *The Turn of the Screw*, and when he was commissioned to write an opera for television in 1966, he decided to use this story. Once again he worked with Myfanwy Piper who did a brilliant job on the libretto. The work was televised on BBC2 in 1971 and a stage version was produced at the Royal Opera House in 1973. The use of tonality and dissonance in Britten's work seems to suit the disturbing and off-kilter narratives of Henry James most admirably.

The joy of these two stories lies in their challenge to the intellect and the sensational way in which the author uses the English language to convey his ideas, impressions and opinions.

BIBLIOGRAPHY

Brown, Nicola, Burdett, Carolyn and Thurschwell, Pamela, *The Victorian Supernatural*, Cambridge University Press, 2004

Esch, Deborah and Warren, Jonathan, *The Turn of the Screw*, Norton Critical Editions (second edition), 1999

Gale, Robert L., *A Henry James Encyclopaedia*, Greenwood Press, 1989

Kaplan, Fred, *Henry James: The Imagination of Genius*, Hodder & Stoughton, 1992

Matthiessen, F. O. and Murdock, Kenneth (eds), *The Notebooks of Henry James*, University of Chicago Press, 1981

Wagenknecht, Edward, *The Tales of Henry James*, New York, Frederick Ungar, 1984

BIOGRAPHY

Henry James was born in New York in 1843. By the age of nineteen he had determined to become a writer. He travelled to Europe, writing reviews and submitting short stories to various publications. He produced his first novel, *Watch and Ward*, in 1871. James lived for a time in Paris before moving to London in 1876. He continued his prodigious output of short stories and novels, including *Roderick Hudson* (1875), *The American* (1877), *The Europeans* (1878), *Washington Square* (1880) and *The Aspern Papers* (1888).

In 1897 he moved to Rye in East Sussex, where he bought Lamb House. When World War I broke out, James was not happy with America's reluctance to join the hostilities and became a British citizen in 1915. The following year he was awarded the Order of Merit by King George V. Henry James died of pneumonia in 1916. His ashes were interred at the Cambridge Cemetery in Massachusetts but a memorial stone was placed for him in Poets' Corner in Westminster Abbey in 1976.